EMERALD DEATH

Bill Craig

ABSOLUTELY AMAZING eBOOKS

ABSOLUTELY AMAZING eBOOKS

Published by Whiz Bang LLC, 926 Truman Avenue, Key West, Florida 33040, USA.

For information contact:
Publisher@AbsolutelyAmazingEbooks.com

ISBN-13: 978-1949504071 (Absolutely Amazing Ebooks)
ISBN-10: 1949504077

The fans of the old style of action tales and stories of High Adventure, wherever you are! Enjoy! And my newborn son Jack, the world belongs to you ...

- Bill Craig

IN THE GOLDEN AGE
OF ADVENTURE....

CHAPTER ONE

Africa, 1939

THE YOUNG MAN RAN HIS FINGERS through an unruly mane of light brown hair, brushing it back from his face. From the rail of the tramp steamer he looked out across the waves at the emerald expanse of the African Jungle.

His name was Mike Hannigan, and it had been about three months since he had set foot on dry land. He had hired on the steamer to work as part of the crew in New York. Only after they had cast off had he found out the ship was going to Africa. The Dark Continent had seemed like a good place to get away to, to lose himself.

O'Grady had made it pretty clear what would happen if he remained in New York, especially after Morgan had been killed by Spinnelli. Africa seemed like a place he could start over, a place where nobody knew him.

Just thinking about New York awakened a long dormant vein of paranoia, and the sound of footsteps approaching from behind caused him to spin, his hand dropping to the military flap holster on his belt and the Colt 1911-A1 .45 autoloader that rested there.

It was only Gregor Shotsky, the Russian first mate. "You seem jumpy today, my friend," Gregor grinned at him, flashing a mouthful of white teeth.

"One can't be too careful. You never know when an enemy might surface." Hannigan forced himself to relax, but his blue eyes remained wary.

Gregor leaned over, resting his elbows on the ship's rail. "I know what you are feeling. I left Russia during the revolution. The Romanoff's were on the run, fleeing before

1

the Bolsheviks. The smart ones... we got out before they took over."

"That why you stayed at sea?" Hannigan was surprised by his own interest. He considered Gregor a good friend, yet their acquaintance had never really gotten personal. He knew next to nothing about the wily first mate.

"Ah, I just wanted to see rest of world. This way, I can. How about you?"

"Easy, I'm just the son of a son of a sailor. The sea is in my blood. I always have to see just what lies beyond the horizon."

"What do you think lies out there?" Gregor waved his arm, indicating the approaching verdant coastline.

"Adventure," Hannigan replied, shaking a cigarette from a crumpled pack he kept in the pocket of his shirt. He fished a Zippo lighter from the same pocket and flicked back the cowling, then rubbed his thumb down the striker wheel. He lit the cigarette, then clicked the lighter closed in one fluid motion that ended with the Zippo disappearing back into his pocket.

"You have heard about what is happening in Europe?" Gregor asked, narrowing his eyes.

"You mean Hitler and his Nazi Party? Yeah, I don't think he'll last." Hannigan blew out a cloud of blue smoke. The green coastline was drawing closer and despite his earlier claim of salt water in his veins, he suddenly felt himself yearning for the feel of solid ground beneath his feet.

"That's not what I hear. I hear he is a monster; that his secret police are taking prisoners, doing things to them. He is expanding, trying to make Germany stronger. I fear they might become too strong, my friend," Gregor sighed, shaking his head.

"What happens if they do, Gregor?" Hannigan took another puff on his cigarette.

"The world will be in a lot of trouble I think," Gregor's face was serious as a nun in church.

"Then I guess we'll have to fight him," Hannigan shrugged.

"Just like that?" Gregor looked amused.

"Just like that. You, me a couple of other guys, we'll just head to Germany and kick his Nazi ass all the way back to Berlin. A piece of cake." Hannigan grinned, flipping the remains of his cigarette out into the ocean, watching the red meteor vanish as it touched the waves below.

"Americans. You are certainly full of yourselves," Gregor laughed.

"Maybe, but we've never been whipped yet," Hannigan grinned. It made him look even younger than his eighteen years, more like a little kid despite the week's worth of reddish brown stubble on his chin and cheeks.

"You might want to shave," Gregor nodded at him. "It's very hot in Africa."

"Exactly where are we landing at, Gregor?" Hannigan pulled another Lucky Strike from his crumpled pack of cigarettes. His throat was raw from too much smoking, but something about landfall had triggered a bout of anxiety for which nicotine was the only remedy available.

"Share one of those and I'll tell you," Gregor said, smiling his pearly white grin. Hannigan reached forward, offering him the butt extending from the top of the pack. Gregor took it and sniffed the cigarette as Hannigan slipped the pack back into his shirt pocket. He drew his lighter and fired up both cigarettes.

"So tell." Hannigan flicked the cowling closed on his lighter and dropped it into his pocket.

"The Congo. A little town at the mouth of the Congo River. A piece of advice though, my young friend; never light more than one cigarette at a time. You never know

3

when someone might shoot at the flame." Gregor blew out a cloud of smoke.

"Reasonable advice."

"Mike, do you have any real plan as to what you are going to do once you go ashore?"

"Not really, no. I figured something would turn up though."

"I have a friend. I'll introduce you to him. He might have some sort of work for you." Gregor tapped the ashes off the end of his cigarette.

"What kind of work?" Hannigan asked, warming to the idea.

"Adventurous work. The kind you came all the way to the Dark Continent to find," Gregor replied.

"Ah," Hannigan blew out a cloud of smoke. It would probably involve running guns or something. That wouldn't be too bad, as long as it wasn't killing or running slaves. Even he had a place where he drew the line, though the boys back in New York might not believe it.

It had felt good being at sea, feeling the waves rocking the boat beneath his feet, the smell of the salt air filling his nostrils and lungs. A big change from the city, even though in some ways being on the steamer and part of its crew was a lot like life in the big city, and not always in a good way.

Gregor had been the first of the crewmembers to befriend him, and his staunchest ally when a few had tried to rough him up. The big Russian had taught him even more about fighting dirty than he had already learned on the streets of New York City.

"You seem troubled, Michael." Gregor flicked his cigarette over the side, watching the fiery comet trail it left until it hit the water and vanished in the blink of an eye.

"A little, Gregor." Hannigan flicked away the remainder of his own cigarette.

"Sometimes I wonder if I've chosen the right course for my life,"

"Only time will answer that question, my friend." Gregor flashed his spectacular grin one last time, and then turned and headed below decks. The Russian was probably turning in early in anticipation of a busy day offloading cargo. Hannigan knew that even if he went to his berth, he wouldn't be able to sleep. The excitement of their impending arrival in Africa would keep him awake.

It was amazing really, how much the world had changed in just the past few years; how much his world had changed, since leaving the farm in Indiana, and journeying to the big city. Everything he had experienced had made him a new person, refined him, and forged him into a man. The boy that had run away from the farm south of Greensboro just a few years before was gone. In his place was a young man, one who had tested his wits and his brawn against the gangs of Gotham. Not everyone lived through that trial by fire – Hannigan had laid a few friends in the ground – but he had survived the ordeal that forced him to flee the city, and now here he was, about to step forth on a new land, one he had never dreamed he would see.

It really was a whole new world, and one he was very eager to explore. Sighing, Hannigan turned from the railing and started for the hatch that would take him below decks, when something cut in front of the moon, eclipsing its light. His breath caught in his throat as he watched the shape glide through the night sky: silhouetted by the moonlight was an enormous silvery dirigible. He couldn't see any markings, but the giant airship fired his imagination. What did lie before him?

Only tomorrow would tell.
The airship passed out of sight and he headed for his bunk, ready to see what tomorrow would bring.

CHAPTER TWO

HANNIGAN STOOD ON THE DOCK, his duffle slung over his shoulder, waiting for Gregor. The sun was already hot in the morning sky, the air thick with humidity. Sweat was pouring down his forehead, soaking the dark blue bandanna he had tied around his forehead to absorb it. There was no sign of the Russian. Hannigan had been waiting for more than an hour for his friend; he could wait no longer.

The docks were alive with activity. A mixture of whites and Negroes were busily unloading cargo from the docked freighters. Hannigan ignored them as he carried his duffle towards the main dock.

Gregor had given him a name the night before: Degiorno. Francisco Degiorno. He was supposed to frequent the bar called The Broken Tusk.

Hannigan sighed. He had hoped that Gregor had been serious; that he would truly help him find employment on landing in Africa. Now, it looked like that wasn't going to happen.

As he approached the end of the dock he could see a small mob of children, most of them thin and half-naked. Beggars, the thought jumped to his mind. Families sent their children because they knew that most sailors would take pity on the kids and give them money.

He almost reached into his pocket for some spare change, and then caught himself. That would only encourage them to follow and harass him. If he wanted work from Degiorno, he needed to arrive at The Broken Tusk without a lot of fanfare, especially without his arrival being heralded by an army of children.

Emerald Death

The Broken Tusk took its name from the ivory trade and the hunters who had earned a fortune for distant European monarchs by shooting elephants and then sawing off the tusks. Without the ivory trade, the Congo would have remained a dark, unknown place. But stalking the largest animal on four legs was no mean feat. Only hard men survived the danger and diseases unique to the jungle, soldiers of fortune. These were the kind of men who gathered at a place like The Broken Tusk.

There were places like that in New York – in every city, he imagined – and he knew how the game was played. Men who needed work done – dangerous work – lurked in such places, waiting for other men who were brave, reckless, or simply desperate enough to take the job, no questions asked. With or without Gregor, he knew work could be found there. Nevertheless, as he took his first steps into a strange land, Hannigan was comforted by the weight of the Colt 1911-A1 stuffed into his waistband underneath the khaki vest he wore.

Despite his excitement over the beginning of a new adventure, Hannigan affected a sour expression. When the first young beggar approached him, Hannigan drew back his fist and made a threatening gesture. The other children shied away and he was able to leave the docks unmolested.

He felt badly for the children. Sure, they were professional beggars, but it bothered him that he had threatened them in order to get them to leave him alone. He would have to do something about that later, after he had secured some sort of employment.

The roar of an engine behind him cut through the usual dockside din and Hannigan spun around to see a Citroen P-45 truck flying towards him. He stared in disbelief for just a moment, and then dived out of the way as the truck shot by. The Citroen skidded to a halt in the dusty street as Hannigan rolled to his feet, his hand slipping under his vest and wrapping around the butt of his Colt. Three men climbed out of the truck – three tough looking men.

"Damn," he whispered. Had Spinnelli tracked him here already? He drew the pistol and leveled it in the direction of the men and they stopped in their tracks. "Can I help you fellas?"

"You Mike Hannigan?" The leader of the three asked. The man was tall and thin, yet his frame appeared to be muscular despite his thinness. Hannigan mentally assigned him the name Thin Man. The other two were black-skinned Africans. One was heavy set, with an enormous gut – Hannigan tagged him with "Jelly Belly" – and the other man he called "Shadow" not because of his dark complexion, but because the man was small enough to vanish in Jelly Belly's shadow.

"Maybe. Depends on who's asking and why." He kept the muzzle of the .45 steady.

"Does the name Francisco Degiorno mean anything to you?"

"Maybe, maybe not." Hannigan shrugged his shoulders but the unblinking eye of the .45's muzzle remained motionless. "Anybody can drop a name."

Thin Man wiped the sweat from his brow. "Gregor called him; told us to pick you up. You were gone from the boat by the time we got there."

Hannigan considered this. Spinnelli's goons might have guessed he'd seek out Degiorno, but they couldn't have known about Gregor, could they? He thought about his friend's absence early on, wondering if perhaps this unsavory trio had beat the information out of the Russian, and then chased him here. Their version seemed a little more plausible, but he remained wary.

"You better be telling the truth." He kept the pistol in hand as he followed the men back to the Citroen. The roof had been cut away, leaving the cab open to the jungle air.

Hannigan climbed into the back where he could keep them covered with the Colt.

His palms were sweating on the knurled grips of the Colt as Thin Man put the Citroen in gear and it started rolling down the street. Hannigan didn't trust any of the three men, but he trusted Gregor, and if the Russian had arranged this, then they were probably square.

~ ~ ~

Gregor Shotsky made his way to the dock. His duties as first mate had kept him aboard The African Queen long after he had thought to leave the ship. The Captain had not been aware that he planned to depart his service on The African Queen on reaching the Dark Continent, and announcing his resignation had further delayed him. He had hoped that Mike Hannigan would be still waiting for him, but he didn't see the American anywhere.

His decision to leave the maritime trade and seek his fortunes on terra firma had been a long time coming. Not long after they left New York City, he had begun planning for the future, making contacts on the ship's short-wave radio. He had eventually reached Francisco Degiorno, a fat Italian crook he had met years before, who had not only promised him work but also asked him to recruit others – sturdy men who wouldn't be afraid to go on a grand adventure. Mike Hannigan had been the only man on the ship that had fit the bill. Hannigan had a sense of adventure and wonder in him like no one else aboard. Gregor could tell that Hannigan wanted to experience life, experience adventure.

Hannigan had a lot of potential. Gregor knew that the American could someday be great in the fullest sense of the word. Patience was his biggest problem; it was something that Mike Hannigan had very little of. He was always ready to move, to see what was over that next horizon. Hannigan had adventure in his blood.

Gregor didn't know exactly what Degiorno wanted men for, but he knew there would be a big payoff involved. He envisioned a search for some legendary treasure deep in the heart of darkest Africa. The thought always brought a chuckle.

He scanned the dock again. Where was Mike Hannigan? Had he already started for The Broken Tusk? Or had something happened to the young American?

~ ~ ~

Mike Hannigan followed the route they were taking, comparing it to the directions that Gregor had given him the night before. Thin Man turned a corner and Hannigan knew that they were not heading for The Broken Tusk.

"Wrong turn, mate." Hannigan jammed the muzzle into the base of Thin Man's skull.

"No it isn't, this is the right way," Thin Man's voice held a quiver as he spoke.

"The Hell you say." Hannigan snapped. "I know where The Broken Tusk is. You have ten seconds to get us back on the right path before my finger pulls this trigger,"

"Pete!" Thin Man said.

Wrong answer, Hannigan thought, and pulled the trigger. Blood and brains sprayed across the windshield and the Citroen lurched as a dead foot pressed down heavily on the gas pedal.

Hannigan swung the pistol at Shadow, who was in the process of drawing his own weapon, and fired. The bullet slammed into his upper chest and drove him backwards, out of the open sided truck and into the street. Jelly Belly made a grab for the wheel, but Thin Man's death stomp had opened the throttle wide; the truck was out of control and headed for a crash. Hannigan jumped up and out of the Citroen, landing painfully on his shoulder and rolling in the dust.

Miraculously he managed to keep his hold on the Colt and watched as the Citroen smashed into a tree, ejecting Jelly Belly from his seat and through the upturned windshield. Blood began spurting from Jelly Belly's neck, but vanished in the cloud of steam that gushed into the air from the shattered radiator.

"First day in Africa and I've already iced three guys," Hannigan muttered morbidly as he picked himself up from the dusty ground, thumbed down the hammer on his Colt and slipped it back into his waistband. "Great way to start the day."

His shoulder throbbed, but it was pain that he could live with. He started back along the way he had come, knowing that it was even more important that he reach his destination. It was evident that someone was trying to keep him from getting to The Broken Tusk. The big questions were who and why?

The only enemies he had were back in New York. There was nobody here in Africa that even knew him aside from Gregor. So why had these men sought him out? It was a question for which he had no answer.

He was more than a little worried about Gregor now. He didn't know who the three men had been, but he was pretty sure they weren't from Degiorno. Did that mean Spinnelli had sent them?

If Spinnelli's wrath reached all the way to the Dark Continent, then Hannigan was in for a world of trouble.

~ ~ ~

He limped back down to the corner, trying to remember the way back to The Broken Tusk, when a tall, pale, thin man with white hair appeared out of a doorway as he passed it. Hannigan's hand almost dropped to the pistol butt, but something about the man's demeanor stopped him. The stranger moved with the certainty of someone that was totally comfortable with his purpose and his abilities.

Hannigan squinted into the sunlight reflecting off the lenses of thin wire-rim glasses.

"Are you okay, My Son?" the man asked. Only then did Hannigan notice the priest's collar around his neck.

"A little bruised, Padre, but doing better than the men that were trying to kill me." He managed a weak grin.

"So I see." The priest replied soberly.

There was a hint of scorn in the priest's manner that made Hannigan feel defensive. "You always this cheerful?"

"Mostly. Sometimes I get so filled with joy I do handsprings."

"Why do I find that hard to believe?" It must have been a joke, but Hannigan didn't feel like laughing.

"I see men like you every day, Son. Men looking to make their fortune, looking for adventure. If they come back at all, they are maimed or disfigured or dead inside. Africa is like no place you have ever been, or seen, or even dreamed of. There are demons here. Heed my warning, Son: this is a deadly dangerous land."

"Thanks, Padre, but I kinda noticed that already. Name's Hannigan, Mike Hannigan." He extended a hand.

The priest looked at it for a long moment then accepted the handclasp. "Father Niles McKenzie. I won't say it's a pleasure to meet you, Mr. Hannigan, but I have a feeling you will make things interesting for a while. I suspect you and trouble are close acquaintances."

"Well, more and more lately, it always seems to know where I am." Hannigan grinned.

"Would you care to confess your sins, Mr. Hannigan?" McKenzie asked softly, his voice almost inaudible.

"I guess God already knows what they are, Padre, without me having to tell him. However, if you can give me directions to The Broken Tusk from here I'd certainly appreciate it."

"The Broken Tusk? Why would you want to go there?" McKenzie asked, more curious than judgmental now.

"Employment. A friend recommended it to me." Hannigan shrugged, wincing slightly.

"Let me guess; you're supposed to talk to a man named Degiorno." McKenzie said it in a way that meant it wasn't a question.

"Yeah, that was who Gregor said to talk to."

"I sense that you are not a bad man, Mr. Hannigan. I must warn you that Degiorno is a truly evil man. You take great risk in working for him, not only to your life but also your immortal soul."

"I need the work, Padre," Hannigan replied. "I guess it's a risk I'll have to take,"

"Then go with God, my Son, and may He always watch over you." McKenzie made the sign of the cross then turned away. Hannigan watched as the priest walked back inside the small white building that he now realized was a church.

Shaking his head, he started back down the road in the direction he hoped would take him to The Broken Tusk.

CHAPTER THREE

THE SUN HAD RISEN HIGHER in the sky and with it came the heat and humidity that heralded the closeness of both the ocean and the jungle. Hannigan's shirt was soaked when he stepped inside the slightly cooler interior of The Broken Tusk. Ceiling fans squeaked lazily as they tried to force the humid air about the dark confines of the bar. Hannigan had automatically stepped to the side of the door after entering so he wouldn't be silhouetted against the rectangular frame of light from the outside. He waited a couple of minutes for his eyes to adjust to the dimness inside the building.

By New York standards, the place was a dive, but Hannigan knew he couldn't afford to be choosey. Besides, he was still wondering about the three men that had tried to kill him earlier, and words of the odd priest he had encountered immediately afterwards; this might be a dangerous place, but it was probably the only place where he was going to get some answers. He managed a confident grin as he approached the bar.

The bartender was a mountain of black muscle; his skin shiny and dark looked almost as if he had been carved from obsidian stone. His dark irises were ringed in white and when he opened his mouth, Hannigan could see that his teeth had been filed to sharp points.

Hannigan blanched; was the man a cannibal? Remembering the .45 tucked under his vest gave him some comfort, but looking at the size of the bartender made him wonder if even the .45 could bring the man down.

The bartender looked down at him. "Yah?"

"Beer," Hannigan replied, trying hard to make sure his voice was steady.

The man nodded and lumbered away. Hannigan eased onto a corner stool so that he could keep an eye on the room. Several tables were filled with a wide variety of tough looking men. Some had the military bearing of soldiers, others just the solid, menacing look of thugs. A multitude of nationalities seemed to be represented in the room – a veritable League of Nations. Hannigan finished his survey as the bartender placed a foam-topped mug in front of him. He dropped a few Belgian francs on the bar and the man nodded and moved away.

As he sipped his beer, Hannigan took another look around the room, and wondered how many of The Broken Tusk's customers were already in Degiorno's employ. He thought about the job Gregor had promised and wondered if it was really as big as promised, but mostly he thought about the man himself; did Degiorno want to hire him, or kill him?

~ ~ ~

Father Niles McKenzie thought about the man he had just met outside the church. His eyes had quickly seen past the façade of bravado the young soldier of fortune wore like a shield. Young Mister Hannigan was a man of destiny, though he wasn't aware of it yet. He reminded McKenzie of another young adventurer he had known during the Great War, his commanding officer Captain Dane Hawkins.

It had been a long time since he had thought about Hawkins and the others, fallen friends and colleagues, ghosts that haunted his dreams and his waking hours besides. The Great War had been terrible, a war to end all wars, they had said of it. Only the end of the war had not brought about safety and security, but an unprecedented time of global strife. The villains had gone to ground, and for more than a decade, the Fighting Hawks had gone after them.

Devil Dog Davis. McKenzie grinned, wondering how the old warhorse was doing. He almost wished he had written, that he had kept in touch with the very few survivors of the old gang. But he had not done so. Instead, he had fled to a remote corner of the world to find a place where he could lay his demons to rest.

Just like Captain Hawkins.

What had happened to Dane Hawkins? McKenzie remembered him as a mere boy, thrust into a role of leadership at far too young an age to handle the burden. As members of their group had died, McKenzie knew that Hawkins carried each death as a personal failure of his leadership abilities, and that he questioned every decision he had made, wondering if perhaps his men might yet live had he chosen a different path. McKenzie, the spiritual leader of the company, had tried on many occasions to get Hawkins to see the truth; that it was war and that even the best laid plans sometimes went awry.

He had failed Hawkins, failed to help him deal with his guilt, until one day the man had just vanished almost as if he had never truly existed.

~ ~ ~

Gregor Shotsky entered The Broken Tusk through a side door, slipping out of the light and pausing to let his eyes adjust to the interior lack thereof. He was relieved to see Mike Hannigan sitting at the bar, quietly sipping a beer and getting the lay of the land. Shotsky smiled to himself; young Hannigan was learning. He made his way to the bar, and dropped his duffle on the floor next to Hannigan's.

"Glad I caught up with you my friend."

"Gregor. I figured you had forgotten about me." Hannigan fired up a Lucky Strike.

Gregor caught the faint tremble in his voice and the way the young man fumbled his cigarette. "What's happened Mike?"

"Trouble." Hannigan took a drink of his beer.

"What kind of trouble?" Gregor's face twisted with concern.

"Three men, claiming to have been sent by your friend, picked me up and tried to take me out in the bush and kill me."

"I'm pleased to see they did not succeed. How did they know to use Francisco's name?"

"That, Gregor, is a very good question." Hannigan shot him a hard look.

"Surely you don't think I had anything to do with it?"

"I'm sure of nothing, which is why I'm asking you now." Hannigan's voice was flat and cold.

Gregor shook his head. "I swear my friend, I have no idea what any of it was about. In fact, I am planning on joining you in working for Francisco."

"Then I guess that just leaves Francisco." Hannigan said, turning slightly on his stool.

"Don't be rash my friend," Shotsky admonished. "I'm sure there is a reasonable explanation."

"Not according to the priest, Father McKenzie. 'A truly evil man,' that's what he said."

An expression of total bafflement crossed Gregor's face. Hired killers? Strange priests with dire warnings?

What kind of deal had he gotten them into?

~ ~ ~

Francisco Degiorno leaned back uncomfortably in the woven wicker high-backed chair. His white suit was stretched tightly across his obese frame. His thick black curly hair was slicked back against his skull. Thick drops of sweat beaded on his brow; even the ceiling fan above did little more than stir the constant hot humid air. He took a white handkerchief and used it to mop away the sweat as he thought about his latest venture.

The Germans had first approached him almost a year before, telling him just enough to get him intrigued. They had spoken of a lost city deep in the heart of Africa, one filled with riches beyond the imagining. Francisco had smiled at the superlative; he had a very active and vivid imagination. So, while helping the Germans with one figurative hand, he had begun planning to beat them to the prize with the other. He had started searching for men – foreigners who wouldn't inadvertently expose his scheme with an offhand comment in the local bars and brothels – who were not afraid of hardship and danger, in order to mount an expedition of his own to search for the lost city ahead of the Germans.

One of his contacts, a Russian named Gregor Shotsky, had promised to try and round him up some men from the crew of the tramp steamer The African Queen. Now that the steamer had finally put into port, the last pieces had been set up on the board; it was time to begin the game.

Degiorno mopped more sweat from his brow, drumming the fingers of his other hand on his desk. Did the Germans suspect at all that he possessed a photographic memory and had recreated the map they had shown him – the map that detailed the city's precise location in the impenetrable jungle – right down to the smallest detail? If they did, then he was most certainly a marked man.

The map currently resided in his safe hidden behind a Monet painting on his wall. Only Lumumba, his trusted lieutenant, who doubled as the bartender in The Broken Tusk, knew of its existence. Most men knew to give the giant African warrior plenty of room. Lumumba would never betray his employer, even under threat of death. But the Germans, with their guns, might not find the big warrior so intimidating. Degiorno was running out of time and he knew it. If he didn't get moving soon, the Germans would have his head. Where was Shotsky?

19

Emerald Death

~ ~ ~

Father Niles McKenzie looked up as a shadow briefly blocked the sunlight streaming through the door.

"Have you gotten all the arrangements made for the supplies, Dad?"

McKenzie couldn't help but smile as he looked at his adopted daughter. Bridget Ellen O'Malley looked so much like her mother she almost seemed a carbon copy. Her long red hair was usually hidden beneath a nun's wimple – a necessary accoutrement given the rough men that lurked about the trading post – but just now she wore it in a ponytail that hung halfway down her back. Her green eyes glowed with an emerald light, an effect that was only accentuated by the smattering of freckles across her sun-bronzed cheeks. She had grown in to a beautiful young woman, and he still wasn't sure when it had happened.

Her parents had died during a cholera epidemic years before and McKenzie had taken his sister's only child in and raised her as if she were his own child rather than his adopted one. He had schooled her in spiritual matters – and not just the teachings of the Church – as well as teaching her to do field surgery and medical work. She was his assistant and good right hand at the Mission. The one thing he couldn't teach her was what it meant to grow up into a young woman. The Congo was a poor finishing school.

"Almost, Bridget. In fact, I'm sure that we have enough, but I'm thinking about riding along on the boat with them this trip."

"Oh really?" she replied, arching an eyebrow at him. She leaned against the wall and crossed her arms.

"Yes really," McKenzie told her.

"And just why would that be?" she asked.

"I want to find out more about someone I met today. A young man, whom I think has a lot of potential for good."

"Another lost soul?" Bridget asked, with a wink. Nevertheless, her curiosity was irrepressible and obvious. "So where did you meet him?"

"Right out front. He took out three men and walked away relatively unharmed."

"Took out? You mean he killed three men right in front of the church? This is the man you're so interested in?"

"Yes. His name's Hannigan."

"Sounds like a real catch." Bridget said half-sarcastically.

McKenzie wasn't fooled. That he had even mentioned the young soldier of fortune was enough; he knew his adopted daughter was interested, and God knew there were few young men he felt worthy of her. He knew her well enough to know that she would like Hannigan, but he wasn't so sure that was a good thing. Still, if he was right about the young man....

"Let's go over to The Broken Tusk," McKenzie told her. "That's where he was headed."

~ ~ ~

Mike Hannigan noted a subtle shift in Gregor Shotsky as a fat man in a white suit entered the bar from a door in the back. He wondered if this was the legendary Francisco Degiorno. The sweating, waddling man didn't look like much of a power broker, to say nothing of Father McKenzie's evil incarnate, but Hannigan had learned that looks could be deceiving. That was just one of the hard lessons Spinnelli had taught him. "That him?"

"Yes," Gregor replied, his face expressionless.

"I got some questions to ask him," Hannigan said, his voice hard and cold.

"Yeah, me too," Gregor answered, his tone matching Hannigan's.

"Gregor! How good to see you," Degiorno called as he crossed the bar. His manner seemed friendly enough; if he was behind the attempt on Hannigan's life, he hid it well.

"Francisco, come join me for a drink," Gregor answered, hiding his anxiety behind a toothy grin.

Hannigan watched the interplay, unimpressed.

"Exactly what I had in mind, old Friend," Degiorno replied with what looked like a sincere smile. "It has been a long time."

"This is my friend, Mike Hannigan. He is interested in working on the job you told me about."

"Ah yes. I was hoping you had been able to recruit some men to help with this endeavor."

Hannigan watched the man's face as he spoke. There was no indication that Degiorno had ever heard of Mike Hannigan before this moment. But if that was the case, how had the three men known to mention his name? What else was going on?

Hannigan shook his head, still trying to figure it all out, but just then the door to The Broken Tusk opened, and he saw something that put the threat of death completely out of his mind. The most beautiful girl he had ever seen in his life stepped across the threshold, followed by the last man he would have expected to find in a dive like this, Father Niles McKenzie.

CHAPTER FOUR

MIKE HANNIGAN HAD JUST REACHED THE PRIEST and the girl when the loud sound of several engines reverberated through the bar. Several of the mercenaries gathered there looked uneasy. Hannigan's attention, however, was fixed only on sight, not sound.

"Hi there, pretty lady, Mike Hannigan at your service," he said gallantly.

"You're Mike Hannigan?" She looked at the priest. "I thought he'd be taller."

"Yes I am Hannigan, and I'm almost six feet tall," he growled.

"From the way Dad described you, I thought you'd be taller," the redhead told him.

"And who might you be?" Hannigan asked, drawing himself up to his full height.

"Bridget Ellen O'Malley if it's any business of yours, which I doubt," she replied with mock haughtiness.

"Hey, you came looking for me, Lady. Not the other way around." Behind him, several of the mercenaries were up and moving, heading out the back door of The Broken Tusk.

"Uh, kids, we don't have time for this right now," Niles McKenzie interjected. Both turned to look at him. "This bar is about to be raided by government troops and they don't look particularly happy."

Gunfire erupted in the street outside as the soldiers spotted the mercenaries trying to escape. Hannigan looked at McKenzie and O'Malley. "The stairs!"

He turned and headed for the steps that led up to the second floor, presumably flophouse suites. He spotted Degiorno and Shotsky moving that way as well. Hannigan was halfway to the stairs when he realized that the priest

23

and his daughter hadn't moved. He turned back to them. "Come on!" he told them.

"Go with him Bridget," McKenzie said, shoving his adopted daughter towards the stairs. "I'll catch up to you,"

"I'm not going to desert you, Dad."

"You're not," McKenzie told her, his eyes urging her to follow Hannigan. "I'll meet you at the Mission."

"Bridget, come with me," Mike Hannigan urged, reaching for her. He caught her hand and drew her along behind him as he climbed the stairs.

"Where are we going?" Bridget asked.

"I have no idea, Bridget, up maybe?" Hannigan told her, still half-dragging her up the stairs.

"Is there another way out of here?" Shotsky asked, spinning Degiorno around to face him. Sweat was pouring down the Italian's face.

"The roof," Degiorno gasped. His bulk was not made for running, especially in the African heat.

"Lead the way," Gregor Shotsky shoved him towards the door.

"Dad," Bridget said, trying to tug loose and head back down the stairs.

"The Padre will be fine, Bridget," Hannigan reassured her. "He wanted me to get you out of here and away from trouble." He wished he were as confident as he sounded. Actually, he had no idea if the priest would escape the raid on the bar. But he intended to make sure that the girl got out and was safe from harm. He followed Shotsky and Degiorno until the four of them burst out onto the roof of The Broken Tusk.

The sunlight was blinding after the dim interior of the bar, forcing Hannigan and the others to squint their eyes in order to see. The gunfire from below was louder now as it echoed up from the street. Hannigan moved to the edge of the roof and peeked over.

The soldiers weren't government troops at all, at least not from the Belgian government. They were wearing khaki uniforms with red armbands emblazoned with a white circle centered below a black swastika. Nazis! Nazis storm troopers were raiding the mercenary meeting place. But what on earth for?

Hannigan ducked back away from the edge of the roof as bullets began to chew at the parapet. He spun towards Shotsky and the fat Italian. "Those are Nazis down there! Does this have to with your big job, Degiorno?" Hannigan crossed the distance in two steps, grabbing the man by the lapels of his white tropical weight suit jacket.

"They want the map!" Degiorno stammered in reply. "I didn't realize that they knew I had made a copy of it. It leads to a hidden treasure deep within the Congo. In pygmy country!"

"Treasure?" the other three asked in unison, disbelief written across their faces.

"A mystic gemstone of some sort." Degiorno replied, his face a beet red.

"They want it for their leader, Adolf Hitler."

"Hitler? That upstart?" Hannigan asked in disbelief.

"He seeks a great many occult artifacts. He apparently believes that with their aid, Nazi Germany will become invincible."

"You seem to know a lot about the guy," Hannigan snarled.

"It's my job to know who I am dealing with," the Italian replied. "Personally, I think the monetary value of the gem far outweighs its alleged mystic value. I want it for the money. That's why I was hiring men to send after it,"

Bullets chopped through the doorway leading to the roof from the bar. "I think maybe we should get the heck out of here," Hannigan said, drawing the Colt from under his vest.

"A sound idea, Michael," Shotsky added.

"Then let's do it!" Hannigan snapped. He fired at the door just as a booted foot sent it swinging open. The Nazi that had kicked it flew backwards into the stairwell. "Run!"

The four ran towards the edge of the roof and jumped into space. Their stomachs lurched as they hung suspended over the long drop then settled with unpleasant abruptness as they landed on the adjacent roof. Hannigan fired out the magazine in his pistol to keep the Nazis down until they reached a door leading down into the building.

Gunfire pummeled the wooden door as Hannigan threw it shut behind him, exploding into splinters as heavy lead slugs chewed it to pieces.

"They must want this mystic rock pretty bad!" He shouted over the din. "Maybe these Nazi guys aren't such pushovers after all!"

He buttoned the magazine out of his Colt and slammed a fresh one home. He was careful to pocket the empty magazine; he had a couple boxes of rounds in his duffel, but he had a feeling finding replacement magazines for the American-made Colt would be next to impossible in Africa.

He charged down the stairs eager to catch the others, but found Bridget stopped behind Gregor and Degiorno who stood arguing in the center of an intersecting hallway.

"We don't have time for this!" he snapped, shouldering his way through them and grabbing Bridget's wrist to drag her along behind him.

~ ~ ~

Bridget gave only a token resistance before following him. So far Mike Hannigan had kept her alive.

Not that she needed any man's help. She didn't have the heart to tell Hannigan – who imagined himself the chivalrous knight, rescuing a damsel in distress – that her adopted father had taught her the mysterious Oriental martial art he called "Te-lo." She could kill with nearly any part of her body if threatened. Still, she liked the young American, and wanted to see what he had in mind.

She was worried about her adopted father, but knew that Niles McKenzie could take care of himself. If anyone could elude the Nazis, it was her dad.

Hannigan kicked open a door and half-dragged her into the room. She could hear shouts from the floors below them and knew that some of the soldiers were entering this building from the ground floor. She shot a glance over her shoulder and saw the other two men following.

Hannigan released his tight grip on her wrist and ran for the balcony. He slipped outside for a moment and then waved for the others to follow. There was a balcony on the next building about six feet away. Bridget risked a glance at the street below. No Nazis yet.

We need to get across this," Hannigan said, upping the safety on his pistol and stuffing it into his waistband.

"How?" Degiorno demanded, gasping for breath.

"Gregor?" Hannigan gave his former shipmate a hard look, and the Russian nodded quickly.

Almost before she realized what was happening, Bridget saw them each grab one of the Italian's arms and run towards the edge of the balcony. She gasped in horror as they threw him over the edge of the balcony.

A loud bleat of fear escaped from the Italian's mouth as he flew through the air and then crashed down on the opposing balcony. Hannigan turned to look at her.

"I don't need any help, thanks." She gave a flip of her ponytail, and then broke into a run and jumped, planting one foot on the balcony rail and pushing off, launching herself into space. She landed on the fat Italian with a thud, driving the breath from his lungs.

At least he makes a soft cushion, she thought with a grin as she rolled off him.

The Russian came next, flying through the air and landing hard on the balcony. Degiorno had crawled out of the way this time. Bridget looked across the space at Mike Hannigan as he charged the edge of the balcony he was on. He got a foot on the rail, just as she and Gregor had done and vaulted into the open.

Except he hadn't jumped far enough, he was falling short of the balcony.

Bridget realized in an instant that he wasn't going to make it and charged to the railing, reaching out to catch Hannigan's wrist in both her hands. His weight threatened to drag her over the rail, but strong hands encircled her waist and held her as she supported Hannigan. His other hand finally caught the rail and she helped him pull himself over it.

"I hate when that happens," Hannigan gasped. Then he looked deep into her eyes. "Thanks, you saved my life."

"Just returning the favor," Bridget replied with a shrug, looking away from his intense gaze.

"Can we move this along?" Shotsky asked, exasperation evident in his tone.

"Good idea," Hannigan said, climbing to his feet. He checked his waistband – miraculously he hadn't lost the Colt – and was distracted just long enough to run headlong into the doorpost. He spat out a curse along with a mouthful of blood from his split lip.

Bridget shook her head in despair. "Mike Hannigan, you have the hardest luck of any man I have ever met."

"Ha! Hardluck Hannigan." Shotsky laughed. "The name suits him."

"Can we get out of here before the Nazis find us?" Degiorno begged, still gasping for breath. The Nazis might not get him, but Bridget wondered if the fat Italian might not end up dying of a heart attack before the day was through.

"Good idea," Hannigan said, pressing a bandana to his mouth as they entered the room. It was deserted, which was a good sign.

If Hannigan's cursed luck doesn't continue to plague us, Bridget thought, this just might work. They could hide out here until the Nazis decided to look somewhere else, and then slip away to her plane. Once there, she could fly them upriver to the Mission, where the Nazis would never think to look. She only hoped her father was meeting with similar success.

CHAPTER FIVE

NILES MCKENZIE FADED INTO THE SHADOWS as the Nazi force crashed into the bar, bristling with weapons. The men fanned out and for a brief moment, he wasn't sure he would be able to hide, but then the gunfire erupted outside and their attention was diverted.

McKenzie slowed his breathing, willing the ambient light to wrap around his form to conceal him in the darkness, becoming a living shadow. He had learned the ancient technique at a Tibetan monastery. The monk that had instructed him had mentioned teaching the technique to one other American, a pilot named Allard who had spent time in the mountains following the Great War, but as far as he knew, no one outside that forbidden place had mastered this ability.

It took only a few moments for the Nazis to divide their numbers, half running back outside, half charging up the stairs. The ones going up concerned him the most; Bridget had gone that way, along with Mike Hannigan and Degiorno.

Cloaked in the concealing shadows, McKenzie moved up the stairs behind the invading force.

He wasn't sure what he would be able to accomplish. He had no weapons; he had forsworn their use following his entering the priesthood. Yet he still practiced the mysterious martial art called "Te-lo." He could, if he chose, kill several of them before they even realized they were under attack, but there were too many for him to kill them all. Besides, killing was something he had hoped never to do again. The faces of those whose lives he had taken during the war still haunted his dreams.

But sometimes there were things worth killing for, worth enduring more ghosts. To protect Bridget, he was more than prepared to kill again, God have mercy on his soul.

The sound of more gunfire – not just the Germans' sub-machine guns, but also the loud report a of big caliber handgun – erupted from above, but it was faint, perhaps originating on the roof. He felt an unaccustomed smile twitch across his lips. So Hannigan had gotten her out of the building and away.

McKenzie faded back into the shadows, becoming one with them, determined to wait the Nazis out. When they left, he would also, and then he would take the boat back to the Mission to rendezvous with his daughter and the others.

~ ~ ~

Sturmscharfuhrer Hans Wessel cursed under his breath as his men spread out across the roof. Degiorno had escaped. The Fuhrer would not be pleased.

Still, he had the original map. He only suspected that the Italian had somehow made a copy of it, he couldn't be sure. Killing Degiorno had simply been a matter of tidying up loose ends.

He removed his brown cap and ran long thin fingers through his thin blond hair, brushing it back from his face. A torrent of perspiration coursed down his high forehead beneath the heat of the African sun. What a forsaken place this is, he thought.

He and his men had arrived the night before after a long voyage aboard the zeppelin *Valkyrie*. Their solemn task was to find the lost city in Africa where the fabled Emerald of Eternity was said to have been entombed eons before. Personally, Wessel felt that the Fuhrer's obsession with this occult relic was ridiculous.

Hitler himself had admitted the truth of Marx's statement, that religion was the opiate of the masses; he manipulated the Church in Germany like a puppet master, promising them a return to the Holy Roman Empire, yet in his private counsels called Christianity a model for Bolshevism. Yet for all his scorn of their faith, he entertained a fascination with the supernatural.

It was Himmler's influence; it had to be. Just as the propaganda minister had filled the nation's head with dreams of the Thousand Year Reich, so too had he played on the Fuhrer's youthful fascination with the ancient mysteries.

Wessel knew of other special teams that had been sent out in search of mythical treasures. Some combed the deserts looking for the fabled lost ark of the Israelites, another group, after receiving special – some would say dubious – information from a psychic medium, had been sent to learn if the so-called Spear of Destiny, which Hitler had personally removed from the Hofmuseum in Vienna and taken to Nuremburg, was actually the lance which had killed Christ.

And now the Emerald of Eternity. Superstitious nonsense.

According to Himmler, the gem was a supposed remnant of the lost city of Atlantis. He shook his head and replaced his cap.

"Recall the men," he announced, sending the command out through the officers.

Degiorno and the others were gone. It would take far too much time and energy to root them out. It would be more prudent, he thought, to simply accomplish the mission: to follow the map to the lost city. If the Italian truly was trying to double-cross them, they could always deal with him later. Perhaps he could spare a couple of agents to stay in town with orders to shoot the Italian on sight.

As eager as he was to return to the *Valkyrie*, he dreaded another encounter with Doctor Ragnarok, the scientist that had been dispatched as the Fuhrer's personal agent in the search, no doubt at Himmler's urging. Or perhaps it was the other way around.

Scientist. The word seemed inappropriate when applied to the masked mystic who seemed to have an almost obsessive interest in finding the stone. Wessel wondered if the good doktor wasn't more interested in finding the gem for his own dark purposes, rather than the glory of the Reich.

Such superstition. It bothered him that so many important decisions – life and death decisions – were being made by men who consulted oracles and the stars. Men like Himmler and Ragnarok, and even Hitler himself. Was the Nazi party truly being led by a madman?

Wessel pushed the thought away as soon as it formed. Such thoughts were the seeds of treason, and the Gestapo had a way of hearing even the faintest whispers of discontent.

Wessel shook his head again. It was time to get back to the *Valkyrie*. He started back down the stairs but as he passed a shadowy corner, he had the strangest feeling that he was being watched.

~ ~ ~

"I'll bet they came in on the zeppelin I saw last night from the ship," Hannigan told the others as they reached the ground floor of the building.

"What zeppelin?" Shotsky asked.

"The one I spotted last night from The African Queen. It flew over right after you went below."

"It has to be Wessel," Degiorno groaned from behind them.

"Who's Wessel?" Bridget asked, turning to face the Italian.

"The German officer who hired me to find The Emerald of Eternity," Degiorno replied with a groan. His white suit was now soaked with sweat.

"What is this Emerald of Eternity?" Bridget asked, her innate curiosity obviously aroused.

"Wessel never told me, but I did some discreet digging. It is a magnificent gemstone, said to have belonged to the most powerful wizard to have ever walked in ancient Atlantis. He used it to see into the future, and with certain rituals, was said to be able to change the future. If you believe that sort of thing."

"And Hitler believes this mumbo-jumbo?" Hannigan asked.

"If it gives him the power to rule the world?" Degiorno shrugged and drew a handkerchief from his jacket pocket to mop his brow. "It's too tempting to pass up."

"You said you just wanted it for the money," Hannigan accused. "Now you're saying this emerald could give him that much power?"

"It could," Degiorno replied, his head hanging low. "He certainly seems to think so."

"You believe in the stone's power," Bridget said. It wasn't a question.

"Yes," the Italian admitted, guiltily. "I've... heard things."

"Then we have to get to it before they do," Hannigan said, his tone grim.

"Yes," Degiorno replied, his voice almost too faint to hear.

~ ~ ~

Captain Morgan raised his cap at the sound of distant gunfire. Damned town was getting too lively for his taste. Getting so a decent riverboat captain can't get no rest when he's in homeport no more. At that moment, a man appeared in front of him.

Morgan's eyes widened in shock. It was McKenzie, the priest from the mission way up on the Congo River. Morgan had loaded his boat up earlier in the day with supplies bound for the Mission, a journey of about two days. He had been planning to leave the following morning.

"Father, what the bleedin' Hell... beg pardon, but what are ye doin' here?"

"Riding with you to the Mission, My Son," Niles McKenzie replied in a solemn voice.

"Bloody Hell you say." Morgan winced again at his use of profanity in the priest's presence, but stood his ground. "I got no room for passengers on my boat. You always fly back with that hellcat daughter of yours."

"Bridget is no hellcat."

McKenzie's voice was soft and low and ominous, and it sent a chill racing down Morgan's spine. If he didn't know better, he would almost have thought the priest was threatening him.

"Eh. Well, when are you plannin' on leaving?"

"Now is fine," McKenzie replied, untying lines and freeing the boat from its moorings. The riverboat was already being tugged into the current as Morgan came to his feet.

"Now wait just one minute, Padre."

The priest turned to face him, the look on his face conveying a promise of a lingering death that would bring more pain than an extended stay in the lowest pit of hell.

"No waiting," McKenzie said, his voice as cold as death itself.

Morgan felt himself swallow a huge lump that had suddenly insinuated itself into his throat. "Right. We'll go now."

He moved to the cabin and fired up the engines. If they ran all through the night, they might reach the falls by late morning. Normally that would be the end of the line for him; the Congo Diamond only ran the lower Congo, while her sister boat, the Congo Ruby, made the long journey between Leopoldville and Stanleyville. But just this once, Morgan thought it might be wise to see the cargo – and the passenger – all the way to the Mission. He didn't want to irritate the strange clergyman any more than he already had. He had already figured it would be smarter to refrain from commenting about the Priest's adopted daughter, if he wished to live.

~ ~ ~

"We have a problem, " Bridget told the others as she led them to where her seaplane – a Grumman JF Duck – was docked.

"What's that?" Hannigan asked.

"The plane only holds the pilot and two other people. There happen to be four of us," she told them.

"Four of us, three seats, yeah that could be a problem, Kid."

"Somebody will have to ride on the outside," Bridget said, her voice grim.

"Gregor, Degiorno. I just drew the short straw," Hannigan's voice was flat and cold, "Get in the plane."

CHAPTER SIX

"HANNIGAN, YOU REALLY CAN'T PLAN to ride outside the plane for the whole flight," Bridget argued.

"You keep the plane low enough so I won't freeze to death and I'll manage just fine," Hannigan replied. His grim expression, cheeks suddenly looking sunken and hollow, gave lie to the confidence behind his words, but his blue eyes peered piercingly at her. "I don't see as how there is any other choice."

Bridget read the seriousness of his intent. "Then you have to let me tie you down," she replied soberly. "I don't even want to think about what could go wrong; the wind could cut off your oxygen and you'd die. We'll have to turn you so you're facing backward."

"I can live with that, Sweet Pea."

Before he could elaborate further, Bridget grabbed him and pulled him close, pressing her lips hard against his. It was an awkward kiss, passionate but clumsy, and it ended as abruptly as it had begun. When she drew back, her eyes were alive with promise. "Mike Hannigan don't you dare die on me."

"Hey, I'm invincible," Hannigan told her, but then as the impact of her offering hit home, he dropped his false bravado, letting his eyes show her his true feelings as well. "I'll make it, Bridget."

"I'll tie him to the strut," Gregor Shotsky inserted. "Trust a sailor to tie the best knots."

"I feel safer already," Hannigan quipped.

Bridget studied the Russian's always smiling countenance. She knew that the two men were friends, but they all owed their present troubles to Shotsky's dealings with the notorious expediter Degiorno. She hoped that

Hannigan wasn't misplacing his faith. She liked the Russian, but she didn't really trust him, and she totally despised Degiorno. The fat Italian she would never trust!

She took a long coil of rope from the cargo box and handed it to the Russian. Then, as Shotsky started trussing Hannigan up like a Christmas goose, she set about getting the Italian into the floatplane.

Bridget positioned him in the observer's pit, but found herself secretly wishing that the men really had drawn lots to see who would ride outside, and that Degiorno had been picked for that dubious honor. She had seen the way the fat Italian eyed her; it left her feeling dirty. She knew that if she ever mentioned it to her adopted father that the Italian would die, mysteriously and probably very painfully. That wasn't something she wanted on her conscience, not just for a look that had made her uncomfortable.

But if the Italian ever laid a finger on her, that would be an entirely different matter.

~ ~ ~

"This what you had in mind when you told me about Degiorno?" Hannigan asked Gregor.

"Not really. When I last knew him, Francisco was into running guns and such. This treasure stuff with the Nazis was a new one on me."

"Those Nazi guys that were after us in the bar were pretty bold." Hannigan ran his fingers through his reddish brown hair.

"The same thought occurred to me," Shotsky replied, suppressing his usual grin "To operate openly in a foreign country, without fear of reprisal? I think the Nazis may prove to be a threat unlike anything the world has ever seen."

"I'm starting to feel that way myself, Gregor." Hannigan tested the rope loop around his waist. "Get these ropes good and tight, I don't want to get beat to death during the flight,"

"Trust me, my friend," Gregor said.

"You know I do, Gregor." He grunted as the Russian cinched the line down. "What do you think of her?"

Gregor threw a glance toward Bridget O'Malley who was pre-flighting the Grumman Duck. "She's a beautiful young girl. But a girl is all she is. Be careful, Mike. Women can often lead otherwise clear-headed men to do foolish things."

"Can't live with 'em, can't live without 'em," Hannigan chuckled as Shotsky pulled the ropes tight. The Russian was true to his word, and Hannigan found it a little hard to breathe, but he knew the ropes would loosen some when they were in the air.

His arms were not secured, and his right hand gripped his pistol as though it were permanently attached. The .45 had a full magazine plus a round in the chamber, and he had reloaded the magazines he had emptied earlier and stowed them in the deep pockets of his vest along with several more. He didn't really anticipate an attack by the Nazis while they were in the air, but he planned to be prepared.

Hannigan was strangely eager to get in the air, to get this ordeal over with. He was using all the bravado he could muster to hide the fear he was feeling. There was a better than even chance that the air pressure alone would beat him to a bloody pulp along the floatplane's fuselage, or that he would end up with broken bones, frostbite or a concussion.

"Seemed like a good idea at the time," he muttered to no one.

Yet, such audacity was the only way they were going to succeed in reaching The Emerald of Eternity ahead of the Nazis.

~ ~ ~

Captain Morgan mopped the sweat from his brow and resettled his Captain's hat on his rumpled gray hair. He hadn't thought it possible, but The Padre was crewing his

41

boat better than his regular bunch. The priest was almost machine-like in his movements and speech, like some sort of futuristic robot he had read about in the pulp magazines.

Something told Morgan that The Padre had been in such tight spots before and had acquitted himself well. The clergyman had a certain air of confidence about him, one that bespoke of a dangerous past. Father McKenzie was a man of action, though he hid it well. Some things were just apparent to those who had been there. Morgan knew that sometimes, violent men chose the cloth as a way of atoning for past transgressions, but McKenzie didn't seem to fit that description. Whatever his story, it was evident in the way he carried himself that the Padre was no stranger to danger.

In their earlier acquaintances, the priest had never spoken of his life before the Mission, and Morgan hadn't asked. A man's business was his own, a dictum the riverboat skipper accepted and appreciated. But now his desire to fill in those blanks was stronger than his capacity for discretion.

"Padre," Morgan asked, "Where did you learn to run a boat like this?"

"During the Great War, Captain Morgan." Father McKenzie replied, staring off into the jungle, but looking, it seemed, at something thousands of miles away. "I learned a lot during that war,"

"I'll bet you did."

~ ~ ~

Although he was as secure as a man ever was, Mike Hannigan held on for dear life as the Grumman Duck began to accelerate along the surface of the Congo River, picking up speed with each second. He had no idea if he would even survive the flight, let alone emerge as the hero he wanted to be, leading the charge against their foes – against the dogs that had tried to murder Bridget.

Bridget.

Hannigan liked Bridget Ellen O'Malley a lot, maybe even loved her a little bit. Maybe even more than a little bit.

He held his breath against the buffeting wind that was slamming him against the hull of the Grumman. It wasn't nearly as bad as he had imagined it would be, but it wasn't exactly a barrel of laughs either. Fortunately, the curve of the fuselage kept the worst of the wind from battering him against the metal frame of the plane.

Hannigan winced as he caught a glimpse of treetops whisking by just below his boots. Bridget was way too low for his liking. Still, he had to admit that she seemed to know what she was doing.

A lot of things had happened since he left New York that fell into the category of things he never dreamed he'd do, but this took the cake: being tied to the side of an airplane flying over the wild jungles of Africa!

Of course he also wouldn't have believed he'd meet a gal like Bridget O'Malley! She was nothing like the flappers and floozies back home – helpless and hapless girls who cared about nothing but themselves. As corny as it sounded, Bridget was the embodiment of his dreams; 100% girl, yet able to hold her own with any guy she came across. Bridget was what his dad would have called a 'top hand' back in the day. He was starting to look forward to spending more time with her, getting to know her better, maybe even ....

Hannigan pushed the thought away. She was easy on the eyes all right, but he had no time for romance. And right now, he was not so much worried about whether she liked him, as he was that she was going to get him killed.

~ ~ ~

Sturmscharfuhrer Hans Wessel hurried his men from the trucks that had carried them back to the airfield where the *Valkyrie* was moored. The huge zeppelin dominated the airfield. The big cigar-shaped hull towered above every other aircraft or structure in sight, and the bright African

43

sun gleamed off the silvery-looking hull of the German airship, making it look like the vengeful spirits that were her namesake.

Valkyrie – LZ 131 – was the pinnacle of German engineering. Powered by four 1,200 horsepower Daimler-Benz diesel engines, she was capable of a ponderous but steady 135 kilometers per hour, and her pressurized hull could take her high above the weather, where the air was too thin for modern airplanes to fly. Three hundred meters long, she was larger even than the mighty *Graf Zeppelin II*, but her lightweight skin of cotton, doped with iron oxide and a substance impregnated with aluminum powder concealed far more than just 250,000 cubic meters of hydrogen gas in twenty individual cells. The *Valkyrie* carried an entire squadron of Messerschmitt Bf 109 fighter planes, which could be launched or landed from the long suspended runway concealed inside the cavernous hull.

Unlike other military dirigibles, which could only carry parasite fighters for their own protection, the *Valkyrie* was the first true aerial aircraft carrier; an airbase in the sky. Fighters could be transported anywhere in the world, flown high above the range of attack planes and anti-aircraft guns, and launched directly on the target, with plenty of fuel and ammunition to ensure victory. With a fleet of airships like her, the Reich would rule the skies, and thence the world.

He wished that his men could spend more time aboard the magnificent ship but Doctor Ragnarok would have none of it. He was totally focused on retrieving the so-called Emerald of Eternity.

He scowled at the thought of his immediate superior. Doctor Ragnarok was a strange one. He wore a steel mask over his head to conceal his true face from everyone. Yet, he had emerged seemingly from nowhere to earn Der Fuhrer's full confidence in matters of the occult.

Rumors had begun circulating among the crew of the *Valkyrie*; rumors that had spread to his own special team of Waffen troopers that attributed the disfigurement to a ritual had gone wrong – a demon he had summoned had melted his face.

Demons. Wessel scoffed at the thought. There was no such thing. No demons, no magic power, no Emerald of Eternity.

If the good doctor's face had actually been melted, it was from some sort of fire, no doubt by some of the strange electronic devices that the man surrounded himself with. Wessel shook his head.

He was an atheist in the truest sense. A pragmatist that believed in nothing he could not see, touch or quantify in some way. He believed only in the one entity that had never disappointed him: himself. Those poor deluded fools who chose to believe in gods, fairies or whatever else, interested him not in the slightest.

Then again, science certainly held its share of strange phenomena. What if the so-called Emerald of Eternity was not a mystic treasure, but simply a physical object with remarkable properties? The debate was irrelevant; he had his orders. Follow the instructions of Doctor Ragnarok, and find the emerald.

Degiorno's escape bothered him more than he cared to admit. The Italian had found allies – mercenaries perhaps – who had proven unusually effective against his men. There was a shrouded corpse in the back of one truck to prove it. The matter was proving to be more than just an annoyance.

As the trucks pulled to a stop, he was surprised to see Ragnarok himself on the ground striding towards him. The sunlight gleamed off the metallic mask, flashing intensely bright.

"Where is the Italian?" Ragnarok demanded as Wessel stepped from the truck. The doctor's voice was as cold and metallic as his visage.

"He escaped," Wessel replied curtly, aggravated with himself for giving his after action report on the tarmac of the airfield.

"How?" Ragnarok asked, his tone conveying his shock. "I thought your men were the best at this?"

"He had help," Wessel snapped. "And I believe that our earlier concerns have proven justified. We need to get airborne if you want to reach the prize before the Italian."

"What have you done?" Ragnarok demanded.

"The Italian has a copy of the map."

"Impossible!" Ragnarok raged. "I hold the only copy,"

"You should have investigated the Italian more thoroughly. I discovered that he is known to have a perfect photographic memory. He no doubt had duplicated the map within hours after we showed it to him. My spies revealed that he has been trying to recruit men for a journey deep within the jungle. I believe he was going to make a try for the emerald," Wessel moved past Ragnarok, eager to take refuge in the zeppelin.

"Stop!" Ragnarok's voiced crashed out behind him.
Wessel froze. It took him a moment to realize he could not move. There was a strange humming all around him; he could hear it and feel it. Mein Gott, he thought, failing the first test of his unbelief by taking refuge in thoughts of the Divine. How is this possible?

"Let me go," Wessel managed to get out between clenched teeth.

"You are sure they are going to go after the emerald?" Ragnarok's voice had taken in the sibilant quality of a snake. Wessel felt his head swivel seemingly of its own volition to look the masked man directly in the eyes.

"Yes!" he hissed, the pain wracking his body almost overwhelming. Then it ceased, gone as immediately as it had come. Wessel felt his muscular control of his body return and the humming vibration was gone.

"What did you do to me?" Wessel croaked, fear filling his body and mind.

"I command your obedience." Ragnarok said imperiously. "You were insolent. Gather your men and make arrangements for us to depart immediately."

"Sieg Heil!" Wessel replied, raising his arm in the traditional Nazi salute. He staggered off, frightened of what had happened, afraid of what Ragnarok was capable of. Wessel waved at his men and they ran for the zeppelin. They had seen Ragnarok's power at work.

Now it wasn't rumor, it was fact!

CHAPTER SEVEN

"WE HAVE TO REACH THE MISSION ahead of Bridget and the others," Niles McKenzie said, wiping the sweat from his brow. He looked over at Captain Morgan.

"Now Padre, if they's a flyin' that plane, there certainly ain't no way for us to get there before them." Morgan reminded him. "At best we might end up a day behind them, depending on if there are people waiting to transfer cargo from this boat to the one above the falls."

"They have no idea what they are getting themselves into, of the danger they will be in," McKenzie muttered almost as if he hadn't heard Morgan. There was a good chance he hadn't. More and more of late, he was having trouble focusing his thoughts. He sometimes wondered if he hadn't been too long in the jungle.

Right now, he had to think about Bridget, about protecting her from the secrets that lay deep in the jungle. He had to prevent her from traveling into Prester John's territory.

The actual location of the legendary Priest King's hidden demesne was but one of many secrets with which he was burdened. For centuries – really since its inception – rumors of the fabled lost Christian Kingdom of Prester John had trickled out of Africa. Rome had long known of his existence, but they conveniently chose to look the other way. Prester John left the Church alone, and they had learned the hard way to leave him alone. McKenzie knew that on several occasions the Holy Roman Order had sent assassins after the immortal Priest King. None of them returned in one piece. The last had been left dismembered in the Pope's own bed while the Pope slept unaware. The message had been received. 'Leave me alone or war will be waged!' Even the mighty Vatican knew when to back off; the cost of an open holy war with the Priest King of legend would have been incalculable. Instead, they had adopted a policy of denial and isolation, which was certainly amenable to Prester John. The College of Cardinals had reluctantly settled for satisfying their unquenchable penchant for meddling by assigning spies to watch from afar – spies like Niles McKenzie. Yet McKenzie did not report everything he learned to his masters.

In his fortress in the lost city of Simbalwe, hidden deep in the reaches of the Congo jungle, the legendary of the Priest King concealed one of the deadliest artifacts known to man: The Emerald of Eternity. He guarded it savagely, as a hyena fights for carrion; it was more important to him than any of his treasures, perhaps more valuable than any other treasure in the world, for the emerald was the key to his immortality. He would kill to keep it – kill at the first hint of a threat to his sole possession. And now Degiorno was poised to take Bridget into the lion's den. If Hannigan and the others insisted on going after it, he would intervene, go himself rather than put Bridget in that kind of danger.

McKenzie thought about that and almost laughed. How much danger did he put her in daily by keeping her here in Africa? Really, what was he doing here at all? Trying to atone for some imagined sins against God or man? God forgave – if he believed anything, he had to believe that – and man simply did not care. So whom did he need forgiveness from? His ghosts?

He felt moisture on his cheeks that wasn't sweat. It took him a moment to realize what it was and where it had come from. Tears. Tears of revelation? Tears of penance? Tears shed for all those he had not been able to help over the years?

You can never run from your ghosts. They always find you. Maybe it was time to leave, time to go back to the States and resume a real life.

McKenzie wiped his face, careful not to let Morgan see what he was doing. He could not afford to show weakness, not now, not in front of the riverboat captain. As circumspect as he knew Morgan to be, rumors had a way of spreading, and he could not afford to be thought of as anything but Father McKenzie, the warrior priest. If it were even whispered that his resolve was flagging, the Mission would become a prime target for the various bands of pirates that operated along the Congo River.

He pulled himself together, straightening his back. He had to focus, focus on catching up with Bridget and the others. He had to reach them before it was too late.

~ ~ ~

Sturmscharfuhrer Hans Wessel peered through one of the sealed portals in the smooth hull of the *Valkyrie*, searching for some sign of the small floatplane that had slipped into the air ahead of him. From this lofty vantage, he commanded a view of hundreds of square kilometers, but the green expanse played tricks on the eye. The jungle hides its secrets well, he thought mordantly.

A thunderous roar shuddered through the zeppelin as two of the Messerschmitt fighter planes blasted down the internal runway and out into the sky. Wessel couldn't help but smile as the fighters came back across the bow in a display of aerial acrobatics. The pilots of the famed Kondor Legion – the Sky Masters – had cut their teeth on the exploits of Richtofen and the Bloody Circus. They were Germany's new best of the best, and couldn't resist a little showing off. They were champing at the bit to prove their steel on the field of combat.

Too bad that their first mission, hunting a lone unarmed float plane, wouldn't provide much sport.

Emerald Death

~ ~ ~

Mike Hannigan squinted at the dots that appeared on the horizon behind them. He had spotted the zeppelin early on, rising lazily like a second moon from the verdant horizon. He wasn't too concerned about that; there was no way the ponderous gasbag would be able to catch them. It was the smaller shapes that had him worried. They were zigzagging across the sky, and growing larger with each passing second. It didn't take a gemstone with magic powers to divine their intentions. As the dots grew bigger, he recognized them for what they were: fighter planes. Things were about to get very hairy.

The planes were still barely larger than buzzing flies in the distance when they swung into line and began driving straight toward the floatplane. Hannigan spied a flickering light emanating from the pursuing aircraft, yet it wasn't until he saw white streaks zipping through the sky that he realized what was happening: the Nazi fighter planes had opened fire!

Hannigan drew his Colt as he tried even harder to make himself a part of the Duck's fuselage. Tracer rounds burned past him; close, too close. Something sparked off a wingtip, a scratch only, but nonetheless, a hit.

Bridget reacted like someone stung by a wasp; sending the floatplane in what felt like a panic climb higher into the sky. Hannigan's stomach dropped and he involuntary clutched at the smooth exterior of the plane for a moment. The fighters however, easily mimicked the maneuver, and continued to close the gap.

Hannigan, feeling a little like David with his sling, leveled the Colt towards the approaching warplane and thumbed down the safety. Locking his elbow, he took careful aim and pulled the trigger again and again. The closest plane suddenly swerved away and Hannigan swore he saw glass on the cockpit shatter.

Then he saw nothing but sky as Bridget threw the Duck into a gut-wrenching loop and barrel roll trying to evade the gunfire from the second fighter. Hannigan tried to aim at the Messerschmitt, but Bridget's acrobatics had put the fuselage of the Duck between him and it. So he did the one thing he could: he held on for dear life!

~ ~ ~

Bridget was a much better pilot than Hannigan could have conceived. While she was no combat veteran, she had learned her skills, not just from her father, who was an adequate aviator, but also from a former ace who had fought in the Great War, and retired to Africa. His stories of dogfights over the fields of Europe had inspired her to practice and learn a repertoire of daredevil stunts, which she used to entertain native children whenever an occasion arose.

Still, it was a lot different when bullets were bouncing off the wings.

"Holy Mary!" she had exclaimed as the first volley sparked off the edge of the wing. Someone was shooting at them.

Instinctively she had sent the plane climbing higher into the sky, racking her brain to come up with a survival strategy. It wasn't until she heard a loud popping noise from the tail of the Grumman that she remembered Hannigan, tied to the fuselage near the tail.

He's shooting back! For all the good it will do.

She looped, diving back down just as suddenly one of the fighters veered off. She sent the plane into a barrel roll, praying that Hannigan would survive the battering she knew he had to be enduring.

Over the din of the engine, she heard a strange mewling noise from the observer's cockpit; the fat Italian was throwing up. "You're going to clean that up!" she shouted, then threw the Duck into another roll.

Sweat beaded on her forehead as she maneuvered the floatplane in ways it was never meant to be maneuvered. Weaving and sliding from side to side, she could hear Hannigan firing whenever the attacking fighter was where he could aim at it. She breathed a little easier, knowing he was still alive at least for the moment. She let the Duck sideslip to the left, giving Hannigan a better angle, but knowing also that he would be completely exposed to the enemy fire.

Suddenly there was an explosion behind her. She sent the plane into a loop and watched in amazement as the Messerschmitt plunged into the jungle, and erupted in a ball of fire. Breathing a sigh of relief, she began searching for a stretch of river to land on.

She had to know if Mike Hannigan was okay.

~ ~ ~

Hannigan nearly lost his grip on the Colt as the Duck went into a roll and looped. His stomach was in his throat as Bridget took the plane through a dizzying dance of evasive maneuvers. Her antics succeeded in sparing them from the fighter's machine guns, but had the unfortunate side-effect of alternately slamming Hannigan against the hard outer skin of the Grumman and throwing him against the ropes, so that he could almost feel the fibers cutting into his skin. He hoped that Gregor had done a really good job of tying those knots; his life depended on it.

Suddenly the Duck slipped left, putting the cockpit of the attacking Messerschmitt in his sights. Hannigan fired out the magazine, and was amazed to see one of the propeller blades snap off. The cockpit's windscreen shattered and suddenly the fighter was a ball of flames plummeting like a fiery meteor into the green carpet below.

Hannigan breathed a sigh of relief. It was only then that he realized that the slide of his Colt was locked open over an empty chamber. With shaking hands he drew a full magazine from his pocket and buttoned out the empty, carefully catching and stowing it, before sliding the fresh magazine into place. He hit the slide release to chamber the top round so that the weapon would be ready for the next crisis. Upping the safety, Hannigan shoved the pistol back into his waistband. His movements were very methodical and deliberate, as if to prove to himself that he wasn't rattled by the near death experience.

Nevertheless, as the Duck dropped towards the river, he wondered if Bridget would think it unmanly if he were to faint.

~ ~ ~

Wessel watched in shock as the second fighter trailed a plume of smoke down into the jungle and a fireball erupted into the air from the emerald jungle below. He lowered the binoculars, shock evident on his face.

"Launch more fighters, "he told his aide, in a hoarse whisper. "Launch the whole squadron."

Although the fighter pilots were not directly under his command, their loss was a stunning blow. Worse, he could feel Ragnarok standing nearby, the sorcerer-scientist's eyes burning into him.

"What has happened?"

"They shot down the fighters," Wessel announced, numb with shock.

"You said that their ship wasn't armed," Ragnarok reminded him, his voice hard edged. "How then is this possible?"

"I don't know!" Wessel was almost frantic. "Perhaps they are very lucky. Why don't you use your magic to find an answer?"

"Are you raising your voice to me?" Ragnarok's voice sounded all the more deadly for its calm quiet.

"Nein, Herr Doktor," Wessel answered quickly, fearfully. He secretly wished that he could just draw the

Lugar 9mm from his belt and shoot the man in the head. But as tempting as the idea seemed, he wasn't sure if it would actually kill Ragnarok, or what the Fuhrer would do when he learned of it. Hitler was as likely to send him to one of the work camps where the Jews were being rounded up for disposal.

Wessel shook his head in frustration at this second defeat in a day's time, and returned to scanning the horizon to watch their enemies' progress. Suddenly the floatplane disappeared from view, dropping into the embrace of the jungle somewhere ahead.

"They have gone to ground," Wessel announced.

"Tell the squadron to stand down," Ragnarok directed. "We cannot afford to waste time chasing after this rabble. But I warn you, do not make the mistake of underestimating them again, Herr Sturmscharfuhrer. You and your countrymen are too arrogant by far. The tiniest insect may kill a strong man with a single bite.

"It has been a long time since I have faced such adversaries. Not since Captain Dane Hawkins and the Fighting Hawks have I faced such adversaries. They had the luck of the gods themselves. They cost me my face."

"Sir?" Wessel was shocked by the admission.

"I didn't always wear a mask to hide my features," Ragnarok replied, his voice distant as if he were remembering. Not until the day I met Captain Hawkins and his men ...

~ ~ ~

Ragnarok spun towards the door of the room he was hiding in an instant before it burst inward. The young man that stood in the door was muscular beneath the tight leather flying clothing he wore, and while Ragnarok did not fear mere physical strength, he was wary of this man who was no more than a boy, with the bright blue eyes that glittered like polar chips beneath dark eyebrows.

"Hawkins!" Ragnarok roared. He summoned his mystical energy, drawing it into his fist.

"I mean to stop you, Ragnarok! I won't allow you to destroy the ship!" Hawkins' voice was as flat and cold as the blade of guillotine. Ragnarok clenched his fist, letting the power build in his body – a spell of power that would burn his foe's bones to dust within his body – but before he could release it, Hawkins had crossed the room and slammed a fist across his jaw. Ragnarok flew backward and the power he had summoned dissipating like so much spilled milk as his concentration fractured. He fell to the deck of the passenger liner, groaning in pain.

His weakness surprised him; it had been a long time since he had taken a mortal form. Hawkins moved in closer. Ragnarok summoned a blast of energy – relatively mild for its hastiness – and sent it snaking from his hands to the American interloper that had emerged to foil his plans.

Hawkins flew backwards, his brown hair standing on end, and hit the deck, but just as quickly rolled and sprang to his feet with a pistol in his hand. It fired just as Ragnarok raised his hands.

Flame erupted around the mystic, a supernova in the tiny passenger berth. Hawkins jumped back, his eyebrows singed by the heat as Ragnarok ran for the door, then gripped the railing and plummeted over into the sea below...

~ ~ ~

"Hawkins nearly destroyed me. The people in that plane, they are of the same sort. If we catch them, we kill them immediately," Ragnarok told him.

Hans Wessel nodded in agreement. "I plan to destroy them if we catch them," Wessel said.

"We cannot allow them to reach the Emerald of Eternity before we do!" Ragnarok insisted.

"They won't," Wessel replied between clenched teeth.

Emerald Death

"If they do," Ragnarok stated, matter-of-factly, "you shall die."

"They won't!" Wessel hissed through teeth clenched so hard they hurt.

CHAPTER EIGHT

MIKE HANNIGAN STEPPED AWAY from the plane on wobbly legs. Once he was a safe distance from the edge of the river, he dropped to his knees and kept his head down until the urge to vomit passed. After several long minutes, he felt someone's presence behind him. Hannigan looked over his shoulder. Gregor Shotsky stood there. "You okay?"

"As well as expected after being tossed around like a bird in a hurricane while being shot at by fighter planes," he shrugged weakly.

"Always the joker, Michael." Shotsky's voice dropped, his tone becoming solemn. "The girl, she worries for you. If you are ready, you should go back to the plane and let her know you are okay."

"Right," Hannigan tried to climb to his feet but he found that his legs still felt like India rubber. Shotsky reached down and slipped his hands under Hannigan's arms and hauled him to his feet.

"Thanks, Gregor." His legs weren't shaking quite as badly now. Maybe the adrenaline rush that had fueled his actions in the air was finally wearing off.

"It is nothing, Michael," Shotsky waved away the thanks. "What you did was very brave. Very stupid, but brave."

"No argument there, Pal," Hannigan managed to grin.

Bridget was working under a steel panel she had raised to reveal the engine of the Grumman Duck. Hannigan noted that there were several large dents in the cover. "So is this what you do for fun out here?" he quipped.

She glanced over her shoulder at him. "You still look a little green, Hardluck."

He grinned. "Yeah well my Ma always said green was my

color."

"Too bad she can't see you now, or better yet, when Gregor untied you."

"Yeah, well, she's been gone a long time anyway." A shadow passed over his face, eclipsing his grin for just a moment, but he shook it off. "That was some slam bang flying back there."

"Slam bang, yeah I bet that's what you were doing all over my plane. Slamming and banging against the fuselage."

"It was worth it Bridget. You're safe. That's what matters the most to me."

"Listen Hardluck, don't go all mushy on me. We saved each other's life; it happens a lot out here."

"Why do you keep calling me that?"

"Calling you what?"

"Hardluck."

"Because you have the hardest luck of any man I have ever met! If it were not for bad luck, Mike Hannigan, you wouldn't have any!" She winked, to let him know that she was only joking...mostly.

"'Hardluck Hannigan;' now why do I have a feeling I'll be living up to that name all my life?" he asked.

"Hmm, maybe because it suits you?" Bridget asked, rolling her eyes.

"Could be," he grinned.

"We were damned lucky none of their hits penetrated the engine cowling. Otherwise this trip might not have had the happy ending it has so far."

"Yeah. I wonder how much time we have before the Nazi zeppelin catches up with us?" Hannigan asked.

"With any luck they won't see us at all. Where I landed, we have a pretty thick canopy of jungle overhead. The trees really grow out over the river here," Bridget replied.

"Is the engine okay then?" he asked.

"It's as good as a new one," Bridget replied.

"You know I want to kiss you, right?" Hannigan asked.

"I know you want to use a toothbrush before you try it," She replied with a grin.

"As long as you know," he grinned back.

"After you use a toothbrush," she smiled back and it was a smile full of promise.

"I can live with that," Hannigan grinned.

~ ~ ~

Doctor Ragnarok scanned the jungle below as the zeppelin moved deeper into the Congo basin. It had been years since he had thought of Captain Dane Hawkins, the man responsible for his disfigurement. It had shocked him when Hawkins had drawn a pistol as opposed to the antique hatchet he normally carried. The pistol had been totally out of character for the American. The bullet had counter-acted his warding and turned the spell he had been casting back in on himself. It was something he should have foreseen, but he had not. Instead it had cost him his human face and locked him into a mortal body. The Emerald of Eternity was his only chance to free himself from his fleshy prison.

The Emerald of Eternity had been created in Atlantis before the dawn of recorded time. The greatest wizard in Atlantis, Oshram Kadella, had not only created the emerald, but had stored in it the life force of ten thousand people, enough to make him immortal. Ironically, immortality had not been Kadella's goal; he knew the toll that magic was taking on his body, on his soul, so he had taken it and fled Atlantis, vanishing into the jungles of a giant uncharted continent: Africa.

It had taken Ragnarok more than two millennia to track the emerald down. Now, it was within his grasp once more and he would not allow it to escape him again. Captain Hawkins had stopped him the last time... Hawkins, who had been a constant thorn in his side. Ragnarok dropped into a seat and looked backwards in time...

Emerald Death

~ ~ ~

Paris, France 1925

Among the elite of Paris, he was known as Dr. Alfred Rodgers, an expatriate scholar, combing the archives of the Sorbonne for esoteric knowledge. Only his acolytes knew his true identity. But somehow, a stranger had found him.

Ragnarok spun towards the door of the laboratory as it crashed open. A man stood there, a brown leather pilot's jacket hanging open over a black turtleneck shirt, dark brown jodhpurs tucked into knee-high jackboots. His dark brown hair was cropped close to his skull giving it almost the appearance of a dark skullcap. "Ragnarok!" the man said, and it sounded like an accusation.

"Who are you?" Ragnarok asked, shocked at the man's impudence.

"I'm the guy they sent to stop you!" the man snapped, stepping into room.

"Come no closer," Ragnarok said, picking up a beaker and drawing back as if to throw it. The man whipped something from off his belt and hurled it in less than an eye blink. Pain erupted from the hand holding the beaker, accompanied by the sound of shattering glass and the splash of liquid raining down on the floor. Ragnarok looked at his hand, his eyes growing wide. Three of his fingers were missing and the flesh of his hand was bubbling and melting away. He could hear someone screaming, and almost laughed at their misery before he realized it was him. Then a fist slammed into his face, throwing him backwards.

It was only after he had hit the ground that he saw the nametag emblazoned across the left breast of the pilot's jacket. Hawkins. Focusing his energy, Ragnarok channeled it through his ruined hand, healing the wounds as a burst of magical energy blasted towards the intruder. The red bolt of energy struck the intruder in the chest and rocked him backward.

But the strange attacker wasn't out of the fight by any means. He grabbed a steel chair and sent it flying with unfailing accuracy, to slam Ragnarok backward against the wall. It was only then he saw the hatchet embedded just above where he lay, still dripping red gore. That was what the intruder had thrown at him that had cut off his fingers and ruined his hand.

Anger boiled up in him. He would have his revenge!

Power blasted out from his good hand, knocking Hawkins across the room. Two other men entered, one a giant, the other shorter and whipcord thin. The giant roared and charged across the room. Ragnarok fed on his anger, using it to draw power from the air around him. He focused it into something hot and hateful, and then blasted it out at the charging giant. The man crashed into and through the wall, sending up a cloud of plaster dust and splinters. But the clumsy attack had been merely a diversion, distracting his attention from the third member of the group.

The smaller thin man moved forward chanting something. Ragnarok fired a second blast, but instead of vaporizing the man, it harmlessly dissipated against a mystical shield that had sprung up between them.

That caught Ragnarok completely by surprise. "How?"

"My secret," the thin man replied grimly. Suddenly something slammed into Ragnarok from behind, arms like steel bands encircled his chest, squeezing with almost superhuman strength, driving the very air from his lungs. Ragnarok struggled, but being unable to breathe, his struggles were weakening.

The thin man was chanting again. Ragnarok could feel the power building around him, but it wasn't enough... not nearly enough.

How did they do this to me? Who are these men?

He focused his thoughts, sending out a blast of power that sent his captor flying back across the room and knocking the thin man to the floor. But the counterattack had done little more than stun the men. He was too weak to keep fighting for the moment. He had to escape! He had to flee!

~ ~ ~

Ragnarok pushed the memories away. He clenched his fist; it had taken several years for him to regenerate the missing fingers. Human flesh was a prison that held him bound until death – and he was very hard to kill – but without corporeal form he was utterly powerless. He had worn many coats of flesh throughout the ages, taking human form or putting it aside at a whim, but this body had been cursed with particularly bad luck. His soul and this weakly flesh had been fused together by the disruption of his own power when Hawkins and his men attacked. He wondered if Captain Hawkins had emerged from his self-imposed exile to plague him once more. If so, this time the outcome would be far different!

~ ~ ~

Mike Hannigan watched from beneath the tree canopy as the zeppelin floated past overhead, driven by the propellers of four enormous engines mounted around its prodigious girth. They didn't dare attempt another flight. Hopefully, the Nazis believed they were dead or stranded with mechanical difficulties. He didn't think he'd be quite so lucky if they encountered more fighter planes.

After it passed, Hannigan went to join Shotsky, who stood over Degiorno as he redrew the map to the lost city from memory. He wondered what they would find there.

Hannigan was surprised by his interest. He had never cared that much about such things – moldy old ruins and such – when he had been in school. History had never been his strongest subject. But a lost city...? Mysteries hidden beneath the mists of time? The prospect of possibly finding some long lost treasure was strangely exciting, like something out of a dime novel, and him the hero of the hunt. It was stirring his blood in a strange way that wasn't at all unpleasant.

Hannigan glanced over a shoulder to where the copper-haired pilot was still tending to her plane.

Maybe it wasn't the treasure hunt that was stirring his blood after all.

CHAPTER NINE

NILES MCKENZIE LOOKED UP as a shadow passed over the water. The big silver cigar shape of the zeppelin floated past overhead, its altitude low enough that he could easily distinguish the red, white and black Nazi emblem on its tail fins. McKenzie had a bad feeling about the airship. It was a symbol of the new Germany – a nation built by a fiendish demagogue who had masterfully played on the fears and prejudices of Germans still smarting from economic collapse that had followed their defeat in the Great War. There had been others like this Hitler – criminals and false messiahs, who had tried to seize power in the early days after the War, and some of them doubtless would have succeeded in their schemes if not for the bravery of Captain Hawkins and his men. Now Hawkins was gone and there was no one left to battle this insidious enemy. McKenzie felt almost as if the silvery airship was a ghost from his past, reaching out to draw him once more into the struggle.

He could feel his heart beating faster at the thought. A part of him was excited by the thought, but part of him was appalled. Did he truly miss the danger; the excitement; the rush of adrenaline? McKenzie hated to think so. He wanted the peaceful life of a missionary and teacher.

Or did he?

McKenzie didn't often think about the old days; those memories summoned the ghosts. And yet, the ghosts had only come after the fighting was done. When he and Hawkins and the others had fought their way around the globe, as tragic as some of the battles had been, he had been able to endure and drive on. It was only when the Fighting Hawks had been disbanded and scattered to the Four Winds that the dreams had begun. Perhaps that was what the ghosts were trying to tell him: never stop fighting. Maybe the best way to honor their memory was to keep the war alive, even if it meant more sacrifices.

Of course, there was Bridget's welfare to consider. She needed to be moved back to civilization, to a place where she didn't have to live in fear of wild animals and wilder men, or of terrible diseases that could strike without warning and disfigure, paralyze or kill their victims. More than that, she needed a real family, real friends – something he could never give her.

It might be better if he went back to what he had once been, a warrior cleric like the Templars of old. Better for himself, better for Bridget, better maybe for the world. Yet, he hesitated. He had worked so long to become the person he now was – a good person, the person he wanted to be – could he give that up? Could he be that person, and still be the warrior priest? It was an absurd notion; change without change.

He gazed up again at the retreating zeppelin. Perhaps the decision would be made for him.

~ ~ ~

Bridget Ellen O'Malley watched Mike Hannigan from a distance as he and the Russian made plans, and just now, that was where she wanted to keep things: at a distance.

She was puzzled by her feelings for Hannigan. Just a glance from him sent warm sensations flowing to parts of her body that embarrassed her. She had never been with a man, but nonetheless recognized the stirrings of desire – "lust," her adopted father would call it. She was aware of her naiveté; not only was she inexperienced in matters of the heart (or was this simply a matter of the flesh?) but she had never gotten so close to any man the way she had with Hannigan in the past few hours. She tried to hide her feelings behind sarcasm, but wondered whom she was really trying to hide from.

I've fallen in love with Mike Hannigan.

The realization came like a rap of knuckles on the head of a wayward child.

A rational voice inside tried to protest, but her heart won out; I'm in love, she thought. And I love this feeling.

She had to know whether this was a mutual attraction, or just unrequited infatuation, but how to find out? She knew it wouldn't do to just blurt out a proclamation of undying love; that would most likely scare him off. No, she had to figure out a way to make sure that Hannigan felt the same for her, that he wanted her as badly as she did him.

She shook her head. She certainly couldn't discuss the subject with her adopted father. But there was one of the village women, Nekoosa, who might have some advice. Nekoosa had been her nanny since her parents had died – not quite a mother figure to McKenzie's fatherly role, but the closest thing to it – and she had taught Bridget what to expect as her body had ripened from that of a young girl into that of a young woman. Yes, Nekoosa would be able to advise her on how to act upon her feelings once they had reached the Mission.

An unconscious smile cracked her determined expression as she continued pretending to tinker with the engine. Yet beneath the flutter of her heart, there was another voice spinning dire alternatives. Hannigan might not even reciprocate her feelings; she might be nothing more to him than a conquest and a night of distraction. He was an adventurer, looking for excitement and buried treasure, not a lover or wife. Indeed, she wasn't competing with another woman for his affections; her rival was the Emerald of Eternity.

~ ~ ~

"So do you still think Degiorno can be trusted?" Hannigan asked, wiping the sweat from his brow.

"That is a very good question, my friend." Gregor shrugged. "Once, I trusted him implicitly. Now... well, I do not know. I am tempted to say 'not at all.' He wants the treasure, so he will be as honest as he needs to be to get it."

"I had a feeling you were gonna say that."

Gregor spread his hands. "You asked. I gave you the truth."

"That doesn't make it any easier to swallow."

"There is a proverb, my friend. 'Keep your friends close and your enemies closer.'"

Hannigan scratched his light brown mane. "Which is Degiorno?"

"Exactly. We will keep him very close; close enough that he will not be able to stab us in the back."

"I'm still more worried about those Nazis. After all, they have the original map."

"Good news, boys," Bridget Ellen O'Malley said as she walked up to them. "I've checked the plane over good. Except for some scratches along the top edge of one wing, she's unharmed."

"That's good to know." Hannigan replied earnestly, not taking his eyes off of her. He seemed on the verge of saying something more, but instead his speechless stare grew into an uncomfortably long silence.

Bridget blushed beneath her freckles, unable to match her green eyes to his blue. For his part, Hannigan felt his pulse start racing; he hadn't felt this nervous since just before the big high school dance.

Shotsky rolled his eyes. "How long before we can take off?"

"We can take off any time we want, but the moment we do, we'll be waving a red flag. That zeppelin probably has radar, and if they pick us up, it's a sure bet they'll send more fighters after us. If that happens, I don't think we can afford to count on Mike to shoot them down this time. Surprise and dumb luck can only carry you so far." Bridget's tone stopped just short of disparaging Hannigan's earlier heroics.

"Mike there has done okay." Shotsky grinned, recognizing the (probably subconscious) motive for her diatribe.

"Mike is lucky he isn't dead!" Bridget replied, her cheeks flushing and her voice rising. "Lord knows he should be. What happened up there was about the only good luck I have seen him have."

"Actually, I've one other piece of good luck," Hannigan intoned.

"Really?" she asked, arching one eyebrow at him. "What was that?"

He took her shoulder and gently turned her until they were face to face. Then he slid his arms around her and drew her body against him, feeling her curves molding to his body as his lips found hers in a long passionate kiss. When he broke the kiss, they were both left gasping for breath.

"Wow!" Bridget gasped, staggering slightly.

"Wow is right," Hannigan agreed.

"You two need to get a room," Gregor's expression was one of mock disapproval. "Soon."

"Gregor, go check on Degiorno," Hannigan growled.

The Russian laughed and walked away whistling a cheery tune. Mike Hannigan looked at Bridget and this time her emerald eyes did not look away.

"Where were we?" she asked, smiling a smile that turned his insides to Jell-O. Hannigan took her in his arms once more.

~ ~ ~

Hans Wessel stared out the porthole at the verdant expanse of jungle below them. It looked nothing like the carefully drawn lines that decorated the antique parchment that was their only guide. That was the bad part of surveying the jungle from so high up. The muddy brown thread that was the river often vanished beneath the canopy of trees for several miles before emerging again. There was no guarantee that the river you spotted was the same one you had been following.

He had tried comparing the map to the official survey of the region. Not surprisingly, the respective representations bore little similarity to one another. The course of tributaries could change without notice due to a fallen tree or boulder that might dam the river and change its course. The map to the lost city had about as much in common with the official charts as the maps available to Columbus had with the Mercator Projection. Well, he thought with a chuckle. They have one thing in common. Here there be monsters....

He had already run into his share of monsters. Somewhere down there were the four that had escaped them in town. Their victory, albeit a small one in the grand scheme, was nevertheless like grit in the gears of his pride. The only way to begin remedying that was to make them pay; he vowed that their debt would be settled through a long and painful accounting.

Nevertheless, the mercenaries helping the Italian were not his foremost concern, not the biggest monster on his horizon. That dubious distinction belonged to someone much closer: the good Doctor Ragnarok.

What concerned him most about Ragnarok was the degree of control the sorcerer had over the mission, and by extension, Wessel's own destiny. To the masked mystic, he and his commandoes, along with the *Valkyrie* and the Messerschmitt fighter planes of the famed Kondor Legion, were but pawns on a game board. As an officer and a fighting man, Wessel knew that sometimes war was exactly like that, a grand game of chess, but the power to command men to go to their deaths ought to have been given to someone trained in military strategy, not to a superstitious wizard with no battlefield experience whatsoever.

Now two of the pilots were dead and their planes lost, and for what? Some fabled lost city and a treasure that could grant immortality. He shook his head. Fairy tales, and valuable resources were being directed into finding them rather than making Germany stronger. The Reich needed men and money, not fairy tales if it were to conquer the world.

~ ~ ~

The sun was sinking low on the horizon and darkness was already falling within the jungle as Captain Morgan guided the riverboat up the middle of the river channel. They were still a few hours from the thunderous cataract known as Livingstone Falls. Barring any sort of problem, he anticipated reaching the portage sometime early in the morning.

That was the easy part of the journey. The lower Congo region was fairly pacified. It was the upper reaches of the river where trouble seemed to lurk around every bend. The inherent danger of the long river journey was part and parcel of the reason Morgan left that part of his business to younger, more adventurous men.

"What do you hear about the pirates, Padre?"

McKenzie stared into the darkening jungle as if lost in thought. "So far they have left the Mission alone, but even I have no idea how long that will last."

"Maybe you should consider arming your flock. I know a fellow who could get you a good deal on some Springfield rifles. Old war surplus."

"I can't do that, Captain." McKenzie offered a look of earnest remorse at refusing the offer. "The Force Publique would never permit native laborers to form a militia. We'd be in more danger from the authorities than the pirates."

Morgan laid one finger alongside his nose. "What they don't

know..."

McKenzie chuckled. "It's a matter of principle," he replied softly.

"Guess then you are doin' what you gotta do, Padre." Morgan knew he was right, and knew that McKenzie knew it to.

Principle, he thought, taking a pipe and pouch from his back pocket. He dipped the bowl of the pipe into the tobacco, tamped it and lit it with a wooden match. Damned foolishness is what it is.

"Dad!" a voice called out from shore, snatching the captain's attention.

"Bridget?" McKenzie called back.

Morgan squinted his eyes; he still couldn't make out the source of the female voice, the jungle and the river could certainly make things tricky, but there was no doubt concerning the identity of the speaker.

"Over here," the voice called again, and this time Morgan saw a flash of light. The small flicker of flame from a cigarette lighter caught his attention. He pointed towards it, letting McKenzie follow his finger.

"Thank God," McKenzie gasped.

Coming from him, the invocation seemed to carry a lot more weight.

CHAPTER TEN

MIKE HANNIGAN HAD A SMALL FIRE going by the time Morgan and McKenzie reached the shore. The fire had helped guide them in to the bank. McKenzie looked relieved as he stepped ashore and folded Bridget into his arms. Hannigan felt a slight twinge of jealousy as he watched their reunion; he was Bridget's protector now. But McKenzie was her father and a priest to boot.

A smile crept across his face as he remembered the past couple of hours in the jungle as he and Bridget had become much more intimately acquainted. Not in a biblical sense, but a lot of time spent necking. It had been paradise, the whole world forgotten except for the two of them. Then Bridget had heard the riverboat's engine approaching. Worried that it might be some of the infamous river pirates that plagued the Congo region, they had slipped to the riverbank to check it out. Then Bridget had recognized the boat that routinely carried supplies to the Mission.

McKenzie's concerned look snapped Hannigan back to the present. The priest's eyes were narrowed and appraising. Hannigan rose to his full height to greet the Priest on equal footing.

McKenzie stopped in front of him. "Bridget says you've saved her life a couple of times now."

"She's saved mine too," Hannigan answered with a shrug.

McKenzie was unimpressed. "I misjudged you, Mr. Hannigan. I had hoped that given the choice, you would choose the righteous path, leading my daughter away from these dangerous men, instead of drawing her into their company."

"I saved her from those Nazis."

"I'm not talking about the Germans. I'm talking about the Italian and your mercenary friend. This ends now. I will not permit Bridget to take you men up river." McKenzie's voice was unequivocal.

"Isn't that her choice to make?" Hannigan asked softly.

"Yes, it is, Dad," Bridget interrupted from behind the priest. McKenzie spun around to face her.

"No, it's not, Bridget. I'm your father. It's far too dangerous for you to continue this foolishness," McKenzie said firmly, almost as if he expected Bridget Ellen O'Malley to play the shrinking violet.

"I'm not a kid anymore Dad," Bridget snapped, her green eyes flashing angrily. "I'm a grown woman and it's time for me to start making my own decisions about my life. I'm going with Hannigan!"

"Bridget, listen to me." McKenzie's tone changed, softening in an attempt to defuse the fire of her temper before it exploded completely and irrevocably. "You have no idea what you are getting yourself into."

"You sound like you know what we'll find," Bridget hissed between clenched teeth, ignoring his efforts. "Maybe you'd like to share?"

Hannigan for once chose the smart course and kept his mouth shut. It hadn't occurred to him that the priest might know something about their quest, but when McKenzie reflexively glanced over his shoulder at him, Hannigan knew there was a lot more to the story than he had first suspected.

"You can tell me now," Bridget persisted, "or we can find out for ourselves... the hard way."

"Saints preserve us." McKenzie growled. "You are asking me to break a sacred vow, to reveal one of the Church's greatest and deadliest secrets."

Hannigan fought to keep his face an expressionless mask. Deadliest secrets? What the Hell was going on?

"Unless you give me a really good reason not to," Bridget said firmly, "I'm going with Mike and the others,"

"Where are the others?" McKenzie asked, noticing for the first time that the Russian and the Italian were nowhere to be seen.

"They're around the bend with the plane," Hannigan said. At that moment, Captain Morgan came running up.

"We need to get back to the boat. I hear engines coming across the water," he gasped for breath. Bridget and McKenzie looked at each other.

"Pirates!" They said in unison. The four of them ran for the small skiff and piled in. Hannigan and Morgan snatched up oars and began rowing away from the shore.

~ ~ ~

The king of Belgium might have claimed ownership of the Congo region, but those who resided in the rain forest and river basin knew that there, a different monarch ruled the river. From the earliest days of European commerce on the Dark Continent, there had been bandits and river-highwaymen lurking in the shadows, but for several years now, the brigands had been marshaled into an indomitable armada under the leadership of a single, almost legendary villain. The authorities could not defeat them; it was easier to simply pay them off for safe passage. Those who did not bargain for the pirates' "protection" were liable for a merciless reprisal if they dared to attempt passage. They were called "the Ninety-Nine" and they ruled the Congo River, the Ninety-Nine and Johannes Krieger.

Hiram Secord was not numbered among the uppermost ten of the Ninety-Nine, but he was ambitious and it looked as though his star was finally rising. Earlier in the week, he had led a small band of renegades to the Lower Congo – an area where the Ninety-Nine had not previously tried to assert their influence – and had captured a riverboat and its cargo. It was a bold move; this far from Krieger's secret headquarters, he and his men were cut off from any kind of support. The course of wisdom would have been to take the booty and withdraw, but Secord's aspirations knew no limits. He had led a second attack, and then another; his audacious goal was nothing less than to establish the power of the Ninety-Nine on the Lower Congo, and thereafter to take his place at Krieger's right hand.

He peered through the near darkness, trying to find a trace of the fire he had seen on shore moments ago. Someone was out there. "Prepare to attack!" he whispered over one shoulder.

He heard a ripple of eager noise behind him as his men locked their rifle bolts or hefted their knives in anticipation of more bloodshed. Secord shared their lust for violence. This was a lot more fun than beating the native laborers on the rubber plantations. He continued scanning the shore and river, gripping the rudder wheel with knuckles white with anticipation, until he saw the shape of a boat looming out of the darkness.

"There!" he hissed, pointing at the squared-off shape gliding across the water in front of them. The men made ready to jump aboard as he guided his boat closer to the target. The cowards had abandoned their boat and taken refuge on shore; this was almost too easy

Suddenly the water exploded into flame! Fire erupted from the surface of the river and it took a moment for Secord and his crew to realize that the source of the flames was petrol floating on the river's surface.

A face, lit up by the orange glow, appeared on the derelict boat and then another, and then a jet of flame lanced toward the pirate boat. Only after the first few of his men had fallen did Secord realize that they were being fired upon.

"Fire!" he shouted and his men opened up on the craft with their Enfield rifles. An inferno erupted from their target and more of his men flew backward, plunging into the black waters of the Congo.

Secord stared in disbelief at the bleeding wounded on his deck and worse, at the gaps in the ranks. One of his senior men, holding pressure on a gushing wound in his upper arm, met his glance with the look of a man betrayed. Secord spun the wheel of his boat, hitting the throttle, goosing it up to full, to get away from the unexpected ambush. The men in the water were goners; the crocs would already have smelled the blood and gone after them.

How had this happened? Who was this enemy that had defied him so, and how had they known he was coming? Secord swore he would find out.

This was not over.

~ ~ ~

Hannigan gripped his .45 and breathed in the smells of burning petroleum, cordite and blood. It was a nauseating odor, but it was also the smell of victory. McKenzie knelt on the aft deck of the riverboat muttering the last rites over one of the pirates that hadn't been dragged off by the crocodiles. Bridget stood amidships, holding an Enfield rifle loosely in her hands, with her head bowed as if in prayer.

The element of surprise had served them well. With Hannigan and Morgan rowing determinedly, it had taken only a couple of minutes to reach the riverboat. The four of them had hurried aboard and Morgan had passed out rifles to Bridget and McKenzie. He had taken the gun reluctantly, but with a sigh of grim determination accepted it and knelt down behind the gunwale.

"We're going to be outnumbered," Hannigan had hissed in the darkness.

"It's too late to run away," the boat's captain had argued.

"That's not what I mean. We need to do something to tip the balance in our favor." He glanced around, looking for inspiration, and when he spied the spare fuel cans, he found it.

Working feverishly, Hannigan had rigged one of the cans into a giant Molotov cocktail, and decanted the rest of the petrol into the water. Then armed with both his trusty .45 and his Zippo lighter, he had crouched behind the low gunwale and waited as the sound of the other boat drew closer.

The battle had been over before it was begun. Although the pirates had superior numbers, the defenders had struck first, slashing their strength by half in the first salvo. Hannigan's field-expedient explosives had taken care of the rest.

Some of the attackers had tumbled off the boat into the black water of the Congo River. Their screams still echoed loudly in Hannigan's ears as he remembered the sight of big Nile crocodiles, drawn by the scent of fresh blood in the water, literally ripping their victims limb from limb in a frothy bloody feeding frenzy. The snuffling grunts of the feeding reptiles and the desperate cries of the dying pirates had sent chills along Hannigan's spine, but the effect on the surviving pirates had been even more dramatic. They had fled.

Hannigan moved to Bridget, enfolding her into his arms as she let the muzzle of the rifle drop to the deck. He touched her chin and raised it so he could look into her eyes "You okay, Kid?"

Bridget's eyes were wet with tears, if they were for the men she had killed or the innocence that she had lost, Hannigan didn't know. He kissed her softly, tasting the tears on her face.

"Yeah, Mike, I, well I just never knew it could be like this," she sobbed. Hannigan hugged her tightly against him.

"We need to get moving," Morgan called from the pilothouse. "We may have licked them, but they'll be back and gunning for revenge."

Hannigan looked at McKenzie. The priest seemed even paler against the darkness, more ghost than human as he nodded his head and went to aid Captain Morgan.

"We're safe," Hannigan whispered as he kissed her forehead. "Things will get better."

"Promise, Mike?" her voice was so quiet he could barely hear her over the engines.

"I promise, Bridget," Hannigan told her, meaning it.

~ ~ ~

Only a few yards away, Niles McKenzie aimed the spotlight out across the black waters of the river, but his eyes were riveted on his daughter and Hannigan.

Though his expression did not show it, he was angry – angrier than he had been in a long time. He had killed men tonight. He knew that it was something that had to be done, but the justifications that good men used to ease their guilt at having to break one of the sacred commandments had long since failed to assuage his conscience. He felt hollow and empty inside, much as he had during the War.

Part of him blamed Mike Hannigan and his friends for forcing his hand and causing him to have to kill, but he knew better. Hannigan hadn't led the pirates here to imperil his daughter. Rather, it was he that had kept her in this violent barbaric place. His insistence on atoning for his past life had placed her in mortal danger. More than that, he had held her back from having a life, and now the fruit of that misdeed was ripening. She was becoming willful, and her naturally rebellious nature was about to launch her on a fool's errand with a rogue – a handsome, charismatic rogue, but a rogue nonetheless.

He had to get her out of this place, away from jungles and pirates, back to the States where she could have a good life. But first, he had to persuade her to abandon the idea of traveling upriver and into the lands ruled by Prester John.

~ ~ ~

Gregor Shotsky snapped to alert when he heard the sound of distant gunfire echoing through the jungle. A lot of gunfire. The silence that followed was even more ominous.

Had the Nazis found them? He looked over to where Degiorno lay sleeping near the fire. The Italian was so worn out from their escape that he slept through the noise, drowning it out with his snores.

The plane was their lifeline; he had to protect it at all costs. Gregor moved towards the Grumman, jumping from the bank onto the float closest to the bank. Ripples spread out across the river from the float.

He remembered seeing an equipment locker in the pilot's well; maybe there would be something there that would prove useful. Clambering up into the cockpit, he began searching. Tucked in with various tools and implements, he found a Very pistol, a type of flare gun, and four flares. It was better than nothing. He loaded one flare into the pistol and stuffed the rest into his pockets, and then scrambled back out of the cockpit. Jumping back to shore, he concealed himself in the shadows and waited, his fist tight around the flare gun's pistol grip.

For several anxious minutes he waited, aiming the Very pistol in at a place on the opposite bank, as the sound of an approaching engine grew steadily louder, until at last, the riverboat came into view.

A spotlight played across the black surface of the river, searching for obstacles that could stave in the bottom of the boat, but Shotsky's gaze was drawn to the two people standing at the front of the boat, backlit in its glare.

Gregor breathed a sigh of relief. It was Hannigan and the girl! He lifted the flare gun and fired.

~ ~ ~

Mike Hannigan laughed as he saw the streak of light from shore followed by the red starburst of the flare. Shotsky was on top of things all right. He turned and waved at Morgan, pointing towards the shore.

The captain stayed with his vessel, while Hannigan and the others climbed into the skiff. Hannigan set the oars and began rowing, quickly bringing them into the marshy shallows.

A familiar voice called from the darkness. "Hardluck, so glad you could join us at last."

Hannigan flashed him a grin back. "Me too, Gregor. Good work, finding that flare gun."

The Russian shrugged his shoulders. "I do what I can."

"We got pirates on our tail. I think we ran them off for tonight, but they might be back."

"What do we do?"

Hannigan glanced at Bridget and McKenzie. "We can defend the boat if the pirates return, but I think Bridget should take the plane on to the Mission."

"Amen," McKenzie added unexpectedly.

Hannigan was expecting Bridget to object, but instead she said only: "I can't take off and land in the dark."

He sighed in defeat. It was going to be a long night. He glanced at McKenzie, remembering the evident remorse the man had exhibited following the firefight with the pirates. "Here's how we'll play this. Gregor and I will row out to the boat and keep watch with Captain Morgan. Padre, you stay here with Bridget and Degiorno."

McKenzie nodded and Bridget, despite the protest in her eyes, held her tongue. Hannigan turned his eyes to the Priest. "First things first, Padre. You know a lot more about what's going on than you've let on. It's time to level with us now. What is out there?"

Emerald Death

"Do you think you are ready for this, Mr. Hannigan?" McKenzie replied soberly. "Ready for the truth? I'll tell you then. There's an army, Mr. Hannigan. An army of the dead!"

Hannigan regarded him with a cool unblinking stare. McKenzie sighed. "Have you ever heard of the legend of Prester John?"

CHAPTER ELEVEN

HANS WESSEL SAT BACK thoughtfully, digesting the news he had just received. He felt his mouth twitch into a half-smile. He had new orders concerning Ragnarok. While the search for the Emerald of Eternity continued, the good doctor would continue to hold supreme authority, but once it was recovered, we would be expendable! Doctor Ragnarok was now under a death sentence.

It seemed that his squandering of two pilots and fighters from the elite Kondor Squadron of the Luftwaffe had caused him to fall out of Hitler's favor. Wessel's new orders called for him to recover the gemstone and then rendezvous with Colonel Wolfgang Kondor.

Kondor was an enigma. The Luftwaffe did not openly acknowledge that such a man even existed and little was known about his history. Nevertheless, an appointment to the Kondor Legion was the most coveted posting a pilot could hope for. Whoever he was, the mysterious Colonel Kondor was refused nothing.

The most noteworthy example was the *Valkyrie* itself. Officially, construction of LZ-131 had been abandoned as aircraft technology had made heavier than air flight more practical, but Kondor had picked up the pieces and finished building the enormous airship in secret. Rumor had it, the *Valkyrie* was the first of a new fleet of zeppelins, and that Kondor was working on a spectacular flying airbase that could constantly provide fuel and repairs to entire fighter wings – all part of a massive unequaled sky armada. With such a force, Germany could rule the skies, and from the skies, the world!

Wessel smiled at the thought, his hand unconsciously dropping to the holstered Lugar on his belt. World domination was a fine goal indeed, but he was more interested in disposing of a certain meddlesome wizard.

~ ~ ~

It was Shotsky of all people who broke the silence to dismissively scoff, "Prester John, the ancient Christian Priest King? He's a legend, nothing more."
Niles McKenzie raised an eyebrow. It was an obscure legend, and he hadn't expected either of the young men to respond in the affirmative. His face remained grim and tight, as did his voice. "No, he is not. I know this for a fact."

Mike Hannigan watched them both, unsure of who to believe or where any of this was going. "I think I missed Sunday school the week they talked about him. Anyone want to bring me up to speed?"

"It is a story the old women tell, Michael. Prester John was the son of Balthazar, one of the three Magi that visited Christ at the Nativity. He's the one who leaves naughty children a lump of coal. According to the stories, Prester John protected a fabulous fortune that was later the envy of Mongol barbarians led by Genghis Khan. In the stories, his kingdom is in the Orient – an island of Christianity amid a sea of Muslims and infidels – but some versions say it is in Africa, Ethiopia to be exact, and that his fortunes remain undiscovered."

"So which is it? Africa or the Orient?"

Shotsky laughed. "Neither. It is a legend, nothing more."

"Prester John is more than just a legend," McKenzie countered. "While it is true that there is a great deal of falsehood in the stories you speak of, Prester John does exist, as does his kingdom – a rogue empire that is Christian in name only. He is here in Africa, in the lost city Simbalwe; the very same city that you now seek."

Hannigan shot him a sharp look. "How do you know what we're looking for?"

McKenzie did not deign to answer. "Prester John will not permit anyone to violate the borders of his kingdom. The Church has tried on several occasions to end his life. Every attempt has failed. In fact, the last assassin sent by the Church? His head ended up in the Pope's bed."

"How typical of Rome," Shotsky sneered. "Your arrogance is without equal. Rather than allow God to decide how he will be worshipped, you send your Inquisitions and assassins to protect your monopoly on faith."

Hannigan raised a hand to thwart Shotsky's rant. "So what happened?"

"They sent me to keep an eye on him," McKenzie said flatly.

"They did that in order to what?" Hannigan asked, rolling his eyes.

"To stop him if he showed any inclination to leave Simbalwe." McKenzie said softly.

"Back up," Bridget interjected. "You're saying Prester John was alive in the time of Christ? So the one here in Africa can't be the same guy. He'd have to be several centuries old by now."

"He was rewarded with long life for his great faith," Shotsky explained in a patronizing voice.

"There's another explanation," Hannigan said. "The Emerald of Eternity."

McKenzie's sharp intake of breath confirmed the statement.

"So the Church knows about the Emerald of Eternity," Hannigan continued. "Do they believe it's real?"

"Very real," McKenzie replied soberly.

"I don't know ..."

"Don't be too sure, Michael," Shotsky offered thoughtfully.

"You were the one telling us it was a fairy tale," Hannigan countered in disbelief.

Shotsky spread his hands apologetically. "Well, most of is rather fantastic. But if such a man did possess the emerald, then a great many things would be explained."

Hannigan shook his head wearily. "Mystic mumbo-jumbo."

"You forget, Michael, until just a few years ago the Czar of my country had as an advisor a powerful sorcerer named Rasputin."

"Sorcerer? The Mad Monk? Rasputin was no wizard, Gregor. He was just a very lucky con man."

"Don't be too sure, Mr. Hannigan." McKenzie's voice was subdued, as if he was more than intimately familiar with the particulars of the case. "To quote the Bard,

'There are more things in heaven and earth than are dreamt of in your philosophy,'"

"But Gregor, do you honestly believe that a gemstone, a rock, can grant eternal life?"

"I have seen a great many things during my life, Michael; some I could explain, others I could not," Gregor shrugged.

"Just because you haven't seen it, Mr. Hannigan, doesn't mean that it isn't real," McKenzie added. "However, there is a great deal more to Prester John than merely the Emerald. He is a very dangerous and powerful entity. He will kill anyone that tries to enter his realm; you are foolish to tempt his wrath, and foolish to attempt to take my daughter along with you."

"What about the Nazis?"

Every head turned to look at Bridget.

"They aren't just a band of treasure hunters traipsing through the jungle. They have resources at their disposal like nothing any of us have ever seen. They want that emerald and they're willing to do anything to get it. Can

Prester John defend himself, or the stone, from those fighter planes? Or from that zeppelin? And if the Nazis get the emerald, then what? I have a feeling we'll all be in a world of hurt."

The passionate argument left the three men speechless for several seconds. Finally, McKenzie broke the silence. "As much as I hate to say it, Bridget, I agree. Prester John may be powerful, but his grasp of technology is mired in the Dark Ages. We cannot stand by and let the Nazis capture the stone."

"We? Then you're going with us, Dad?"

"I don' see that you've left me any choice," McKenzie sighed with resignation.

"But we must move quickly."

Gregor punched Hannigan playfully. "Ready to save the world, Hardluck?"

"Hardluck?" McKenzie raised an eyebrow.

"It's Miss Bridget's pet name for him. Hardluck Hannigan."

"'Hardluck Hannigan,'" McKenzie repeated with a half-smile. "It suits you."

Hannigan shook his head ruefully. "Padre, you don't know me well enough to know just how true that is."

"Bridget, your Dad almost smiled!" Shotsky cried.

"Oh my God! I'll mark it on the calendar," Bridget answered, laughing.

"Friends, I have a host of friends," McKenzie sighed.

~ ~ ~

Hiram Secord looked over his remaining crew. He had lost half of his men in the abortive assault on the riverboat. He had not expected so much resistance from the other craft; no one ever fought back. It had caught him off guard.

The surviving crewmembers were grumbling among themselves, and it was making him nervous. He glanced over his shoulder at where they were huddled at the back of the boat. More than one of them had been giving him pretty evil looks. It was making his stomach churn.

So far, it hadn't gone as far as open mutiny. There was one mate he trusted not to stab him in the back – a face to face cutthroat maybe, but not a backstabber was Black Angus McGuire. McGuire would back him up, at least for a little while longer, and the rest of the men would do what Black Angus told them to do. His only chance at redemption was to lead them on a successful raid against the boat that had defeated them, or else they would feed him to the crocodiles.

~ ~ ~

"So what do we do about the pirates?" Hannigan asked, wiping away a film of sweat from his forehead. Despite the fall of night, the humidity in the jungle was horrible.

"They'll be back, though I think we hurt them pretty badly." McKenzie stroked his chin thoughtfully. "We need to be ready for the worst."

"You seem to have some experience at this sort of thing, Padre. How do you want to handle it?"

"Your original plan was a sound one; you and your friend Gregor join Morgan on the riverboat. Bridget and I will keep an eye on Degiorno."

"Make it both eyes. He's a slippery one."

"I want to have a little talk with Francisco. I'm interested in seeing the map as well. Everything hinges upon it; I want to see how accurate it is, and perhaps figure out where the Nazis obtained it."

"Okay Gregor, let's head for the boat," Hannigan turned and headed towards where they had tied up the rowboat, and Shotsky fell into step beside him.

"Do you trust the priest?" Gregor asked as soon as they were out of earshot.

"About like I trust Degiorno. McKenzie has an agenda of his own, I just haven't figured out what it is yet."

"That is my feeling as well. Is it safe to leave Degiorno with him?"

"Yeah, because I do trust Bridget. I don't believe she will let him steal away with Degiorno. Bridget wants to keep the emerald out of the Nazis hands as bad as we do."

Bridget intercepted them at the rowboat. She stood there, her arms crossed and her foot tapping as she stared at Hannigan. "Where are you headed?" she asked, raising an eyebrow.

"Out to the riverboat," Hannigan replied easily. "Your Dad wants us to help Captain Morgan keep watch in case the river pirates come back."

"You mean he wants you out there and me safely on shore," Bridget replied, exasperation evident in her voice.

"Something like that." Hannigan chuckled. "I don't think he's quite ready to accept that you are a young woman now, and not a little girl."

"Well, Hardluck, I'd say we need to change that notion." Bridget suddenly pressed her body hard against his. His reaction was automatic and left little room for misinterpretation.

Somehow, Hannigan resisted, gently pushing her back. "Down girl. There is a time and a place for everything, this is neither."

"What, I'm not good enough anymore?" Bridget asked petulantly.

"Yes you are. I just don't need to make an enemy of your dad right now. Between the pirates and the Nazis, I've got all the enemies I can handle." He leaned forward and gently kissed her on the lips. "Later," he added in a soft whisper.

"Promise?" she grinned, brushing a stray curl back from her face.

"Promise," Hannigan told her with a smile.

CHAPTER TWELVE

THIN BEAMS OF MOONLIGHT glittered off the black water of the river. Secord had spotted the dim glow of a small fire on shore and was able to spot the riverboat that had gotten away earlier at a terrible cost to his crew. He reached over and tapped Black Angus McGuire on the shoulder, rousing the man from his fitful slumber. McGuire opened his eyes and sat up, giving Secord an evil look.

"What?" McGuire asked, his voice dripping with irritation.

"We found 'em," Secord grinned.

"I'll wake the men. They'll be wantin' a piece of this action," McGuire said softly.

"Sure enough they will," Secord agreed.

As McGuire moved back to rouse the men, Secord checked his revolver, making sure it was fully loaded. He wanted the people on the other riverboat worse than he had ever wanted anything in his life! They had made a total and complete fool of him in front of his men.
Keeping the boat's engine barely above idling speed, he nosed it towards the other boat. They would take care of anyone on shore afterward...

~ ~ ~

Mike Hannigan opened his eyes as an unfamiliar noise intruded on his sleep. He sat up, taking a moment to realize where he was. Then he placed the noise. It was the motor of a boat. Hannigan stood up quickly, clutching his pistol.

"I see them, Michael," Gregor whispered softly from the bow.

"Is Morgan aware that we're about to have guests?" Hannigan asked.

"Don't know, haven't had time to wake him up. Instead, I've been preparing for our guests. Here, take one of these," Gregor handed him a whiskey bottle that felt nearly full. Hannigan noticed a cloth rag stuffed into the top of the bottle. He didn't have to take a whiff to know that the contents were not for human consumption.

"You got one of the rifles?" Hannigan asked.

"Something even better." Gregor grinned. "The Captain had a Thompson submachine gun stowed away along with several drums of ammo. I just happened to find it when I was looking around,"

"Why do I have no doubt you can use it well?" Hannigan asked with a grin.

"My trusting face perhaps?" Gregor grinned back.

"I'll head for the stern and get in position for when they attack."

"I think they are coming now." Gregor jerked back the charging handle on the Thompson as Hannigan snatched up one of the bolt action Enfield rifles and headed for the back of the boat.

The approaching engine roared to full throttle and in the moonlight they could see the pirate boat charging across the water towards them.

Hannigan lifted his rifle and took careful aim at the wheelhouse. The Enfield jumped in his hands and the window at the front of the wheelhouse shattered. The pirate boat swerved, veering slightly until a new hand took the wheel and the advance resumed.

Hannigan could see the pirate crew bunched up along the side of the boat as it rapidly closed the distance. He flicked open the cowling on his lighter and touched the fire to the petrol soaked rag. Staying below the gunwale, Hannigan lofted the Molotov cocktail in a high arc that dropped it right in front of the wheelhouse. The bottle shattered and flames exploded across the deck. Two of the pirates ignited, and ran screaming to dive off the boat, trailing flames behind them as they hit the water. Gregor's bottle hit the deck an instant later, igniting a second conflagration that raced to meet the first.

Hannigan worked the bolt on the Enfield, firing it out before Shotsky got the Thompson into action. He dropped the rifle drawing his Colt, thumbing back the hammer and squeezing the trigger as fast as he could find a target. The screams from the pirate ship were abruptly drowned out as Gregor opened up with the Thompson. The big .240-grain slugs ripped through soft flesh to send gouts of blood hissing into the flames.

The sound brought Morgan running from the wheelhouse, with one of the Enfield Rifles gripped in his fists. He skidded to a stop and fired the Enfield at the pirate boat almost without aiming, yet pirates were falling as he fired. Suddenly the gas tanks on the other ship erupted in a huge mushroom cloud of flame that climbed into the night sky like a premature sunrise. A smell like roasting pork was heavy in the air as burning body parts rained down into the river.

The pirate boat began to list as water washed across the broken deck, then the doomed vessel slid beneath the Congo. Screams of the dead and dying filled the air along with the snuffling grunts of feeding crocodiles. The water looked like a window into Hell itself, reflecting the glow of the fire amid a mosaic of blood and torn limbs. Great clouds of steam erupted into the air as the burning boat vanished under the water. There were a few pirates still thrashing in the water, but they didn't last long; the crocodiles saw to that.

~ ~ ~

Bridget Ellen O'Malley awoke to the sound of gunfire. Jumping to her feet, she started towards the river. A hand landed on her shoulder, spinning her around. "They need my help, Dad!" Bridget snapped.

"No, Bridget, they don't," Niles McKenzie said. "They have the situation well in hand."

"What the devil is going on?" Francisco Degiorno demanded from the far side of the fire. McKenzie had been keeping a close eye on the wily Italian to make sure he didn't slip off into the jungle on his own.

"River pirates, but I'm sure you know all about them," McKenzie replied dryly.

"The Ninety-Nine?" Degiorno asked his voice quaking with fear. It was a rhetorical question, and both men knew it.

"We really can't see all that much from here, just a burning pirate boat sinking into the main channel of the river. Would you like to swim out and see if you recognize any of them?" McKenzie asked. "You heard the shooting and explosions the same as we did."

"Krieger stays off the Lower Congo."

McKenzie raised an eyebrow, as if the comment had confirmed what he already knew to be true. "Maybe these aren't his fellows after all."

"Shouldn't we go help them?" Degiorno asked, trying to muster some small amount of courage to cover the fearful quiver in his voice.

"They have it pretty well taken care of now. The crocs will finish anyone they miss."

"Mother of God!" Degiorno gasped in horror at McKenzie's apparent callousness.

"Hannigan, are you okay?" Bridget's voice rang out. McKenzie spun around his eyes narrowing as he sought out his daughter's slim form in the darkness beyond the fire.

"Can you fly the plane, Padre?" Degiorno's voice asked quietly from behind him. McKenzie turned to face him. It was then he caught sight of the small revolver in the Italian's hand.

"I can," McKenzie replied softly, forcing his body to relax so he wouldn't telegraph his plans to the Italian.

"Then how about the two of us take a ride to get to the emerald ahead of everybody else?" Degiorno moved around the fire, keeping the revolver close to his body.

"How about we don't?" McKenzie asked his voice barely above a whisper.

"I could kill you now, where you stand," Degiorno hissed.

"Maybe," McKenzie said softly. "Maybe not."

Then he vanished. Degiorno's eyes went wide as he searched for the priest. Suddenly something struck his wrist and the revolver flew into the circle of light around the small fire. Fingers as hard as steel bars found pressure points and the Italian was suddenly on the ground moaning with pain. When he opened his eyes, McKenzie was standing over him.

"Are you man or ghost?" Degiorno gasped, eyes wide with an almost primal fear.

"I've seen the evil in your heart, Degiorno. I know what kind of person you are. Never forget that." McKenzie turned and walked over to where the revolver had fallen. He scooped it up and stuffed it into his belt. McKenzie looked down at the Italian. "You won't be needing it anymore."

"God help me," Degiorno gasped, fear taking hold in his heart.

"He's been trying." McKenzie said softly. "But you won't accept his help. I need to check on my daughter. If you move, I will kill you,"

~ ~ ~

Bridget stood near the banks of the river, gazing anxiously out toward Captain Morgan's riverboat. She waited anxiously to hear Hannigan's reply, but all she was hearing so far was shooting. She had retrieved her own pistol from the plane earlier in the evening. It was a Smith & Wesson .38 caliber revolver with a four-inch barrel. The gun was holstered at her waist, but the flap was unsnapped in case she needed the pistol to fend off crocodiles. However, the crocs seemed too engrossed in feasting on the pirates that had either jumped or fallen into the river.

"Hardluck, are you okay?" Bridget screamed out over the river.

"Doin' fine, Kid!" Hannigan's voice carried over the water to her. Bridget's knees went weak and she felt like fainting but didn't. Hannigan was okay! That was the most important thing. She felt a smile creeping across her face.

~ ~ ~

Mike Hannigan heard Bridget shouting for him, demanding to know if he was okay. He shook his head, then called back: "Doin' Fine Kid!" He hoped that would pacify her until the killing was over. He didn't want Bridget to see this part of him, the cold-blooded killer that was more machine than man. He fired his pistol, mercifully killing yet another pirate that was being torn apart by the crocodiles.

He took a deep breath, seeking another target. The river was becoming quiet, the crocs dragging the corpses below the surface to their dens buried deep in the mud. Finally, he looked up at the sky and noticed it was beginning to lighten with the coming of a new day.

CHAPTER THIRTEEN

DOCTOR RAGNAROK STOOD on the control deck of the zeppelin watching as the sun burned into view at the edge of the horizon, emerging from the jungle as if all of Africa were on fire. It was a breath-taking sight; it reminded him of the creation of the universe.

That had been a glorious time – an entire cosmos in chaos. Only later – thousands of years later – had he realized the awful truth: he was imprisoned in the physical realm, modulated in the confining dimensions of a world where everything that is or ever was consists of raw energy and crude matter. Worse, he'd been trapped in the gravity well of this world as it gradually coalesced into a terrestrial sphere; trapped, just as he was trapped in this frail human body.

The reminiscence only further exacerbated his irritation with the current situation. For expediency's sake, he had allowed the Nazis to imagine that he was working for them, serving their ends. To facilitate that deception, he was forced to allow the smug toad Wessel to command the mission, and Wessel seemed to be stalling. He had anchored the zeppelin for the night despite Ragnarok's urging that they press onward. His desire to reach the emerald, to free himself from his fleshy prison, was all consuming. Yet, he could not argue with the toad's logic; in the darkness, they might miss the landmarks to the emerald's location, and only postpone that eagerly anticipated event.

Still, the toad had seemed different; arrogance had replaced the fear that he had instilled in the man earlier. Something had happened outside his influence, something he would have to investigate. First things first, however. It was time to begin moving again, time to go after the Emerald of Eternity. Soon it would be within his grasp.

A noise behind him alerted Ragnarok that the command crew for the airship was arriving from their quarters and he turned to face them. Conversations stopped as the crew saw him standing there waiting for them. They had not expected this; he could feel the fear as they saw him, feel it rising from their weak flesh, filling the air, giving him strength and fresh power. "It's about time you got this ship underway," Ragnarok intoned, his voice deep and intimidating. They scurried to their places like insects. He felt his burned lips turn up slightly into a smile beneath his metal mask.

~ ~ ~

"Okay, Degiorno, it's time to put up or shut up." Hannigan fixed the Italian with a deadly expression. "Draw the copy of the map."

"But ..."

"No buts Francisco," Gregor Shotsky said, his voice devoid of emotion. "Do it now or we'll just shoot you and toss you to the crocs, or better yet, leave you here for the Ninety-Nine to find,"

"Anything but that," Degiorno shivered. Hannigan placed a large piece of paper and a pencil in front of the Italian. McKenzie knelt down beside Degiorno.

"Remember, I know that territory very well," McKenzie said softly, quiet menace flowing off him. The Italian nodded and began to draw. McKenzie watched the map take shape, quickly picking up various landmarks. He had not overstated his familiarity with the region; in fact, he knew exactly where the lost city was located. He was pleased to notice that Degiorno placed the temple of Simbalwe more than twenty miles from where it was actually located. The Nazis were going to the wrong location. In the thick Congo forest, twenty miles might as well be on another continent. McKenzie decided to keep that piece of information to himself for the moment.

Bridget and the others were right in one respect; the Emerald of Eternity could not be allowed to fall into Nazi hands. He would do all that he could to prevent it, but he was not happy about the prospect of having to face Prester John. Prester John was frightening; the limits of his mystical powers untested. The Pope himself was frightened of the Priest King.

~ ~ ~

Mike Hannigan had lost interest in watching Degiorno draw the map and walked out to the river's edge. In less than twenty-four hours time, he had foiled three assassins, escaped from a group of Nazis, fought in a dogfight with German fighter planes, and survived two battles with pirates. Somewhere in between all the violence, he had also met Bridget and fallen in love. It was enough to make his head spin.

In an effort to bring some kind of control back into his life, he set about cleaning his pistol. He had put a lot of lead through the barrel and the mechanism was black with carbon residue. The Colt had taken good care of him, and now it was time to return the favor. He also needed to find some more ammo for the weapon, or soon it would be no more useful than a paperweight. He knew that the Thompson submachine gun Shotsky had found the previous night used .45 ACP ammunition, same as the Colt; with any luck, Captain Morgan might have a few rounds to spare.

As he scraped the gunpowder residue from the mechanism, he kept an eye on McKenzie, as the latter watched Degiorno recreate his map. The Padre's eyes had betrayed him; he had spotted something significant but hadn't spoken up. The good Padre was keeping secrets, that much was very evident, but how to get him to reveal them that was the question. Hannigan didn't doubt that the priest was a good man, but he knew from experience that men who follow God put His interests above all others, even their friends.

After reassembling the big reliable Colt, Hannigan untied the rowboat and stepped inside it, taking an oar and using it to push himself away from shore. It took only a few brief moments of rowing to reach the riverboat.

"Ahoy, Captain!" Hannigan called as he tossed a line onto the deck of the riverboat. "Permission to come aboard?"

Morgan replied with a grin: "Permission granted, Son. You saved both my boat and my ass last night, you're welcome anytime."

"Well, then you won't mind me asking a favor," Hannigan said as he stepped onto the deck.

"Name it."

"Four or five boxes of ammo for my .45 if you can spare it," Hannigan replied. He liked the riverboat captain. The man reminded him of his grandfather who had helmed a riverboat on the great Mississippi River years before.

"Not a problem, Lad. I keep a couple of cases on board for that old Chicago Piano. You're more than welcome to a few boxes." He rustled in a locker and passed over several waxed cartons of Automatic Colt Pistol cartridges, then gave Hannigan an appraising glance. "So you're the fellow sparking the Padre's adopted daughter and getting him all fired up?"

Hannigan raised an eyebrow, a little surprised by the revelation. "He doesn't strike me as particularly 'fired up.'"

Morgan chuckled. "Aye. He was so concerned about little Bridget that he could barely think. She's led a pretty sheltered life out here, but she's a woman with a woman's needs. Ain't many fellows out here with much to offer; the river ages a young man right quick. But you're still pretty fresh. The good father would be a fool not to be a little worried about her virginity."

Hannigan could feel the heat of blood rushing to his face. "Ah well, ok," he stuttered.

~ ~ ~

Gregor Shotsky watched Francisco Degiorno work on the map. He had noticed Hannigan moving off towards the riverbank earlier. McKenzie had drifted away at about the same time. It was then that he had noticed that Degiorno was making some subtle alterations to the map.

Through narrowed eyes he watched as Degiorno shifted landmarks on the map. He kept quiet, but it was something he would mention to both Hannigan and McKenzie later on when the opportunity arose.

"I'm done," Degiorno said firmly as he laid the pencil aside.

"Is it accurate?" Shotsky asked, not really expecting the truth.

"More so than the one the Nazis have. The original was in my safe. They have a copy I substituted when they weren't looking. On their copy everything is off by several miles," Degiorno grinned.

"I'll get the others. McKenzie! Come here, Padre, and take a look at the map," Gregor called, watching Degiorno from the corner of his eye. The man flinched visibly. He was afraid of the wily old priest. McKenzie and Bridget both headed in their direction and he could see Hannigan rowing back to shore. Hannigan would join them soon enough.

Gregor watched as the wiry priest walked over to the Italian. He moved with the grace of a panther. Something was coming to life in the priest, something that had been gone a long time. That much was easily apparent to anyone who watched him move. Bridget had moved up beside the priest, shaking her red curls back out of her face and then tucking her hair behind her ears so she could more easily see the map as well. Being such an accomplished pilot, Gregor had no doubt she could read the chart with the same ease as her father.

After several minutes McKenzie folded the map. "It's pretty accurate as far as the landmarks and the countryside," the Priest said.

"I saw a couple of small things that weren't quite right, but they were not too far off either," Bridget added.

"That's great," Mike Hannigan said, walking up to join the rest of them. "Now we just gotta get us all there."

"Bridget can fly two of us ahead and then come back and pick up the other two," McKenzie folded his arms.

"That would work. The two she comes back for can help Captain Morgan get those supplies loaded on his other boat and headed towards the mission. She should be able to pick us up on the river," Hannigan agreed.

"Degiorno can come with me and Bridget can fly us ahead to the Mission first then," McKenzie said.

"Well, since you have the map, Degiorno can wait with me and Gregor can go with you. He's really good at this expedition stuff. Besides, that way I know you'll send Bridget back for us."

"You don't trust much of anyone, do you Mr. Hannigan?" McKenzie asked with a sigh.

"Not since most of the people I've met since I set foot in Africa have tried to kill me," Hannigan replied.

CHAPTER FOURTEEN

MIKE HANNIGAN WAVED AT BRIDGET as the Duck lifted off. She dipped her wings in response, then the plane climbed into the bright blue morning sky. Hannigan returned his attention to Degiorno.

"Time to do some honest work for a change." He shoved the Italian towards the rowboat.

"The priest is up to something," Degiorno stated as he took a seat. "You know that don't you?"

"Why should he be any different? Listen Pal, I know you altered the map, and I know the Padre knows the territory up there. Do you honestly think he didn't spot the changes you made? I don't trust him any more than I trust you, which is why I sent Gregor with him."

"You trust the Russian?" Degiorno replied in evident surprise.

"Unlike the rest of you jerks, Gregor has never given me a reason not to trust him. Now start rowing." Hannigan shoved the rowboat out into the river and clambered aboard.

The plan was for Bridget to fly her father and Gregor to the mission where she would refuel and then fly back down to the rendezvous in Leopoldville to pick up Hannigan and the Italian. Once they were all at the Mission, the quest for the Emerald of Eternity would begin in earnest.

Morgan stood by, Tommy gun in hand, watching as they made their approach. He kept an eye on Degiorno as the Italian heaved himself over the gunwale, but did not offer a helping hand. Evidently, Degiorno's reputation had preceded him. Hannigan set about securing the rowboat as Morgan sent Degiorno forward to haul in the anchor. A few minutes later, the Congo Ruby was moving upriver towards the falls.

The journey to the rail depot was brief. It was mid-morning when they tied off at the pier and commenced offloading cargo. Hannigan stripped off his shirt as he began the sweaty job of transferring crates onto the rail flats that would eventually be taken on a short journey around the tumbling falls. Time spent under the African sun was bleaching his brown hair blond as well; already thick blond streaks mixed with the reddish-brown. Sunlight glistened off the thin sheen of perspiration that painted his sun-bronzed flesh, accentuating the wiry cords of his physique. Hannigan wasn't muscle-bound in any sense of the word, but his visible musculature was whipcord tough and had a quality of strength beyond the size of the muscles themselves.

Where Degiorno was gasping and wheezing for breath, unaccustomed to hard labor, Hannigan was seasoned from his labors aboard the African Queen.

There were several other riverboat captains gathered on the dock, helping secure other loads bound for other destinations to boats of their own. Hannigan caught a snatch of a conversation as he hauled the last load onto the dock. The silver zeppelin had created quite a stir as it flew overhead the day before, following the course of river, then abruptly turning to the northwest, as if looking for something.

He concealed his pleasure at the news. The Nazis had bought Degiorno's bogus map directions. He eased the crate to the dock and tried to catch more details of the exchange, but instead heard a rough voice from behind.

"Hey Skinny, what tree did they break you off of?"

Calmly, Hannigan turned around to face the man.

"I mean a little branch like you, don't you think you should leave the work to the real men?" The speaker was an impressive looking man. His dark hair was cut in a bristly flat top that reminded Hannigan of porcupine quills, and he was tall, well over the six-foot mark. His shoulders were more than three feet wide and his upper arms were bulging so much that his arms were pushed away from his body. His fists were big and meaty and looked like they could easily fill a gallon bucket. There was a lot of power in those arms, and Hannigan knew he would have to be careful to stay out of their reach.

"You talking to me?" Hannigan asked, letting some of the accent he had learned in Brooklyn creep into his voice, along with the attitude that usually accompanied it.

"I sure am, little boy. What gives you the right to come here and take work away from me?" The big man asked.

"I'd think you got enough work at the zoo, or don't they pay the gorillas over here?" Hannigan grinned at the man, but the humor was not evident in his blue eyes, which were cold and calculating as he measured the man, waiting for him to make the first move.

The man's face went red. "You don't know who you're talking to, do you little boy?"

"Have we ever met before? No, I don't think so. So obviously we've never met and I don't know who you are. How long did it take you to figure it out?" Hannigan snorted derisively.

"Nobody talks to Rhino Hayes that way," the man growled, his voice rumbling out from deep in his chest.

"Rhino? What kind of first name is that? Didn't your parents like you very much?"

"I'm gonna break you in half for that, little boy," Hayes growled, starting forward. He threw a looping left at Hannigan. The latter easily ducked under the swing and shot out with fists to strike two nerve plexus' on Hayes' exposed flank. The big man let out a yowl of pain.

"Tsk tsk, now, you're gonna frighten all the wildlife," Hannigan said, ducking under another lunge and swinging out his leg to trip the bigger man. Hayes crashed to the dock, causing the wooden pier to ripple like an earthquake.

"You're gonna die for that!" Hayes roared, scrambling toward Hannigan.

But the wiry adventurer was quicker . He bounded over Hayes, planting his hands on the man's shoulders as he propelled himself into the air to land directly behind the big longshoreman. Hayes sprawled forward and slammed into a thick piling. The impact snapped it in half.

Hannigan was on him in a flash, steel hard fingers searching out different nerve clusters, pressing hard into them to totally disable the larger man. Howling in frustration, Hayes crumpled to the dock in a heap.

Hannigan looked at the other men. "Anybody else?" he asked, not even breathing hard. The other laborers just looked at him then shook their heads and went back to work. Hannigan retrieved a bucket full of water and tossed it onto his vanquished foe.

Hayes reared up sputtering. "What the bloody hell?"

"You lost, Hayes." Hannigan said softly. "Want a rematch?"

"Not bloody likely, Mate." Hayes rumbled. "You pack a helluva wallop for a little feller."

Hannigan grinned. "Dynamite comes in small packages my friend. You need to be more careful about who you bully."

"I'll take that advice, I think." Hayes extended his hand. "Didn't catch your name."

"Hardluck Hannigan," Hannigan said, using the nickname Bridget had hung on him.

"Rhino Meriwether Hayes," the big man replied, shaking Hannigan's hand. Much to Hannigan's surprise, Hayes didn't try to use a bone-crusher grip on him.

Hannigan thought about his earlier taunt. With a name like Meriwether, no wonder he favored the nickname Rhino. "Who are you working for, Rhino?"

"Nobody at the moment." Hayes responded honestly. "That's why I was picking on you."

"Maybe I can set something up with Captain Morgan. He's a good man and an honest fellow who only expects an honest day's work for an honest day's pay."

"Sounds like a square deal," Hayes replied with a grin. "You hook me up here and you got a friend for life, Hardluck. You ever need me, you just holler real loud."

Hannigan was about to elaborate on the planned upriver journey when, from the corner of his eye, he spotted Degiorno making a couple new friends. Hannigan stopped and Hayes stopped with him. When Degiorno looked over his shoulder and saw Hannigan, he blanched with fear. He quickly said something to the two tough looking laborers with whom he had been speaking, and the men started towards Hannigan, while the weaselly Italian tried to slip away.

"I got them," Rhino Hayes growled, stepping forward. A massive fist swung out and the first of the two went flying through the air. Hannigan darted after the slippery Degiorno as Rhino descended on the second bruiser.

The Italian ran for all he was worth, but Hardluck Hannigan was in better shape and a whole lot younger. Hannigan easily caught him, digging his hands deep into the Italian's shoulders and hauling him backwards.

"That wasn't very nice, Francisco. Do I need to take steps to make sure you don't run again, like shooting your kneecaps?"

"No," Degiorno replied, quavering.

"Good, because I would hate to have to push you through the jungle in a wheelchair. We had a deal to find that damned emerald, right? I expect you to hold up your end of it."

"Yes," Degiorno gasped. "This was just a misunderstanding."

"Let's not misunderstand each other anymore. Otherwise I might have to go ahead and kill you. As it stands, I may yet," Hannigan told him, dragging him by the collar back towards the boat.

Rhino Hayes was standing and waiting, grinning. The local toughs were sprawled senseless on the dock. "So Hardluck, is life always this interesting around you?"

"You have no idea."

CHAPTER FIFTEEN

THE HUMIDITY HAD RISEN with the sun and actually gotten worse as the day progressed. By the time Bridget had landed the Duck at the Mission her clothing was sticking to her, as was McKenzie and Shotsky's. She knew Hannigan and especially Degiorno had to be miserable in the heat and humidity.

As the Duck descended over the river, several of the children from the Mission came running out to the dock to watch the floatplane land, clapping and cheering at the waves made as the floats touched down in the water. They gathered at the dock to greet her and Father McKenzie. Bridget knew most of the kids, having acted as their teacher much of the time. She had nursed many of their parents after various wounds had been received from the overseers on the rubber plantations.

So many were maimed over small slights or made examples of. It sickened her. Especially since they were starting to force the young children to work as well. All for profits. She hated that the children could suffer the same mutilations as their parents, all because some corporation wanted to make a profit.

It ignited a fire within her, one that made her want to fight against the injustices she saw. Except her adopted father refused to let her. "Let it rest Bridget, it's the way things are," McKenzie had told her on more than one occasion. Bridget refused to believe it. Whatever her adopted father had suffered through in the Great War, it still affected him to the point where at times he seemed almost spineless, yet at other times he was as ferocious as a lioness protecting a cub. She wondered if she would ever figure him out. Somehow, a part deep inside her doubted it.

Bridget threw back the hatch and climbed out of the plane, easily clambering down onto the dock ahead of her adoptive father and Gregor Shotsky. The children surrounded her immediately, calling her name. Bridget smiled and knelt down, hugging as many of them as she could. Some of the children called excitedly to her adopted father in their native language and he responded kindly in the same. They asked questions about Gregor Shotsky but she noted that Niles McKenzie shrugged those off without answering. Bridget waved the kids off and settled into the task of refueling the plane so she could go after Hannigan and Degiorno.

~ ~ ~

Father Niles McKenzie quickly dismissed the children and then gave Gregor Shotsky a tour of the Mission, including the small machine shop that he had built for fashioning parts that they couldn't buy for the older floatplane and farm machinery that was used on the Mission grounds.

Gregor thanked the Padre and set to work building the devices that he thought might come in handy for the upcoming expedition. One of the items looked like a steel rod except that when you twisted it, four prongs snapped out of one end to create a grappling hook. The other end twisted off to become a club. Overall it measured about twenty inches in length and was nearly an inch thick. It would make a good truncheon.

Shotsky already had a spool of thin, nearly unbreakable line he had created some time before. He attached it to the grapple and then concealed it in the truncheon end of the club. With practiced moves he screwed the ends together, effectively concealing its purpose. He then set to work on building a second one.

Gregor had also been giving some thought to Hannigan's .45. There might come a time when a need for silence was required, even when a shot needed to be made. He had an idea for creating a small suppressor for the gun, but he would need to wait on Hannigan to fit it properly. Gregor set to work.

~ ~ ~

It didn't take long for Bridget to have the Duck refueled and to get her airborne again. The children waved from the riverbanks as the Duck took to the air once more. Bridget dipped her wings in response. She was on her way back downriver to pick up Mike Hannigan.

Bridget's thoughts drifted to the time they had spent alone in the jungle, the thrills that had raced through her body as Mike Hannigan had made her feel a woman. She ached for the sensation again, hoping that the opportunity would arise before they went after The Emerald of Eternity. Mike Hannigan had taught her much about the arts of love in a short time, and she was now a very eager student! Bridget knew she had pleased him as well, and looked forward to doing so again. She knew that Hannigan could teach her a lot, given the chance. Of course with her adopted father dogging their steps, they might not ever get that chance! Bridget shook the thoughts out of her head and scanned the air around the Duck, making sure that there were no unwelcome visitors coming after her beloved airplane again.

~ ~ ~

Father Niles McKenzie walked to his small office at the rear of the Mission. As he walked, he fished a key from his pocket. His office, Bridget's room, and the storage area were the only doors in the Mission that had locks. McKenzie reached his office, unlocked the door and stepped inside. He took a quick breath and shut the door behind him, shutting out the noise. Without thinking, his fingers turned the lock; he didn't even notice the protective symbols painted on the walls and door and around the windows. They were as much a part of him as his skin.

He had hoped that they would protect him from the demon that had murdered his parents when he was a child. They had been missionaries in India when it had happened.

He could still remember it vividly. They had gone to stay at a remote village just a few kilometers from Delhi. His mother, how beautiful she had been, her long blonde hair streaming down her back, her blues eyes bright with laughter. His father had been a dour man with dark hair and dark eyes. His sister had been left with the housekeeper back in Delhi. They had settled into the grass-thatched hut where they would be spending the night, the small fire in the center of the hut providing the only illumination. McKenzie had been almost asleep when the shadows had thickened and taken shape, attacking his parents and savaging them. He had curled into a fetal ball, hearing their screams long after their voices had fallen silent. On that night Niles McKenzie had vowed to fight Evil in all of its forms!

He knew that someday, the demons that had killed his parents would come after him. So Niles McKenzie had prepared himself, studying not only Christianity but magic as well, becoming acquainted not only with white magic, but dark magic as well. He had been better versed in the days when he had fought beside Dane Hawkins and Mad Dog Davis during the Great War. His body was a weapon as well in those days. He still worked out every day, doing katas in the art of Te-lo. He could perform the deadly art effortlessly, even though he had tried to eliminate killing from everything he did.

He had killed too often in his past and his dreams were often haunted by the faces of the men he had killed during the Great War, haunted as well by the faces of friends who had died fighting as part of the Fighting Hawks.

McKenzie wondered again what had ever become of Dane Hawkins himself. The leader of the Fighting Hawks, what had happened to him after the war? The last he had heard, Hawkins was hiring himself out to go on expeditions into dangerous areas of the world; areas that any sane man would avoid like the plague. Still, that was Hawkins' choice.

Hawkins seemed to be trying to prove something, as if the man's war record wasn't enough. He was forcing himself to live up to an ideal that was so far above realistic it wasn't funny. McKenzie had tried on more than one occasion to counsel his former leader, but Hawkins had no desire to listen. He was a man beset with inner demons, ones that could only be conquered by his own will. Except McKenzie wasn't sure that Hawkins' will was strong enough.

Towards the end of the Great War, Dane Hawkins had become more and more reclusive. More standoffish to those who had been his closest companions. Dane Hawkins was a man on the edge of insanity. Niles McKenzie could only hope that his former commander had not succumbed to the insanity.

McKenzie pushed away the thoughts of the past. He had to concentrate on the present. Protecting Bridget was at the forefront of his thoughts. Saving her from the fury of Prester John was his most immediate concern. Because there would be fury when the Priest King found that they had invaded his domain, no matter what the cause. He would be no less angry that they were after the source of his immortality.

Prester John would kill them all without a second thought if it suited his purpose. Prester John had the idea that the church had abandoned him. He felt threatened by the Church, felt like they were out to assassinate him. The sad part was, Prester John was right. The Church did want to assassinate him. He was a threat to them, especially given his prolonged life. It was a secret that the church coveted and condemned at the same time. Putting an end to the Priest King and recovering The Emerald of Eternity would do much to enhance his own reputation in The Church, removing the blight on his record from his war years and his use of dark magics to help vanquish Evil.

McKenzie had long ago decided that sometimes using the methods of Evil to defeat it worked the best. That had certainly proven the case with Doctor Ragnarok and other assorted villains that the Fighting Hawks had faced over the years. He opened the small safe in his sanctuary and removed a small amulet. It was made of moonstone and silver and held a great deal of power. He had acquired it in Ireland from a Druid Priest. It had helped him defeat Doctor Ragnarok.

He hoped it would work as well against Prester John.

~ ~ ~

Mike Hannigan grinned as he spied the Grumman Duck dropping out of the blue sky towards the river. Rhino Hayes walked up beside him to watch the silver floatplane come in for a landing. "Is that your girl?" Hayes asked.

"Yeah, she is," Hannigan grinned. He looked over his shoulder towards where the Italian sat slumped against the bulkhead of the cabin. "Hey, Degiorno, get your sorry butt moving. Our ride is here," Hannigan yelled, his tone commanding.

"That one is gonna give you trouble, Hardluck," Hayes said looking back at the soaking wet and hopelessly rumpled Italian. The former crime boss looked more like a wartime refugee at the moment.

"I'm counting on it, Rhino. I don't trust him as far as I could toss this boat. He's a weasel, but at the moment, he holds the clues to something I want," Hannigan replied.

"Well good luck, Hardluck. Hopefully things go your way. One day we will meet again, I think," Rhino Hayes said, taking Hannigan's hand in his massive paw and shaking it.

"I hope you're right, pal," Hannigan release his hand and then raised it to wave at Bridget as she taxied the Duck up close to Captain Morgan's riverboat. Hannigan glanced over his shoulder. Degiorno was still slumped against the bulkhead glaring at him defiantly. Hannigan whirled and crossed the space between them with five long strides his hands reaching down and gathering in the material of the Italian's jacket. Hannigan yanked the man to his feet and bodily propelled him towards Rhino Hayes.

Hayes caught Degiorno's staggering form and flung him through the air the distance to crash down atop the fuselage of the Duck. Hannigan ran towards Hayes and the man lifted him, tossing him through the air like he was nothing. Hannigan had been expecting it, however, and was able to get his feet under him and made a catlike landing on the wing.

As nimbly as a tightrope walker in a circus, Hannigan skipped up the wing and grabbed Degiorno's collar. With seemingly very little effort he lifted the Italian off the fuselage and dangled him over the muddy waters of the Congo. Hannigan's blue eyes stared deep into the Italian's brown fear-filled eyes. "Are you going to cooperate better or do I just drop you into the river for the crocs?" Hannigan asked, his tone as cold and bleak as an arctic winter.

"Yes, I'll cooperate!" Degiorno screamed, his voice very high-pitched with fear.

"Good, 'cause the crocs on this side of the waterfall haven't eaten as well as their cousins downstream lately," Hannigan replied, shoving the man into the cockpit. Hannigan climbed in as well and pulled the hatch closed above him.

Emerald Death

"That was quite a display, Hardluck. Sure you aren't using too much luck up?" Bridget asked teasingly.

"Only time will tell," Hannigan grinned back at her. Bridget flashed him a smile and turned back to the controls, taxiing the Duck away from the riverboat and turning it around to have a better longer stretch of river to use for takeoff. She engaged the throttle and the plane leaped forward, the pontoon landing gear sending up huge sprays of water from each side, then the plane was skipping over the surface and finally lifting up into the air, climbing into the bright blue sky.

CHAPTER SIXTEEN

NILES MCKENZIE AND GREGOR SHOTSKY were both waiting at the dock when Bridget brought the Duck in for a landing. The two men had struck up a brief if grudging friendship, especially when Shotsky had shown McKenzie some of his makeshift creations. Even McKenzie had been impressed by both the practicality and the innovativeness of the devices. The fact that they were fairly concealable in their true purposes by their appearance was also impressive.

McKenzie felt a grimness settle over him. It was a familiar sensation, one he had felt many times over the years. He was girding himself for battle with forces that he knew were capable of destroying not only his life but his soul as well. His normally dour demeanor became even more so. McKenzie checked his vest and the pockets sewn into it. The vest was of a special design that he had come up with during the Great War and his time with the Fighting Hawks. Vials of holy water were secured in canvas loops sewn across the chest pockets; other mystical talismans were carried in select pockets as well as both a small prayer book and a book of both offensive and defensive spells. It had been many years since McKenzie had actually practiced magic, but he hoped that it was a skill he hadn't forgotten.

Fighting Evil during the Great War had been more than just facing the Huns. There had been so many different faces worn by Satan's agents over the years. Some had been conquered by mortal means, others through spiritual or magical means. Somehow, the Fighting Hawks had managed to defeat them all. But it had come at a great cost, not only physically and mentally, but spiritually as well.

McKenzie himself had fled to darkest Africa to work for the redemption of his own soul. Mad Dog Davis had retreated to the coast of Maine and the North woods, and Captain Dane Hawkins had become an explorer and vanished off the face of the Earth.

McKenzie waited patiently as Bridget taxied the Duck to the dock. He almost smiled at the thought. Duck to the dock, it was amusing. He and the Russian moved quickly to toss ropes from the dock to the plane and quickly had the craft moored almost before the hatch slid back and Bridget and the others left the plane. Bridget and Hannigan both looked almost way too happy. The Italian, however, looked totally miserable. He actually even looked thinner, his clothing now hanging much more loosely than it had a couple of days before.

"He looks a little worse for wear," McKenzie nodded, indicating Degiorno.

"He wasn't really prepared for honest work," Hannigan replied, his hand finding Bridget's and their fingers entwined.

"He was pretty tame on the flight from the boat. But then I imagine flying through the air without a plane can have that effect," Bridget said mischievously

"How did that happen?" McKenzie asked, curious.

"While boarding," Bridget explained, deliberately being vague. McKenzie shook his head in wonder. It seemed a lot was going on without his knowledge. Maybe even more than he wanted to know.

"Yeah the Italian got his first flying lesson," Hannigan deadpanned.

"We have most of the supplies loaded onto the old floatplane, but we need to put a few in the Duck," McKenzie said.

"Then let's get moving," Hardluck Hannigan growled.

~ ~ ~

The silver zeppelin hung in the air, barely obscured by clouds, waiting and watching like some great predatory bird, searching for some sign of the others seeking its treasure. The *Valkyrie* was ready to attack, poised and waiting for a sign of the others seeking the treasure that had thus far been denied it.

The waiting was the hardest part for the crew, who were growing more nervous around Ragnarok with each passing minute. It was evident to everyone that Doctor Ragnarok was quickly descending into some sort of strange madness as they waited for some sign of the Italian who had stolen the real map to the temple where The Emerald of Eternity rested.

Hans Wessel hated waiting, especially with a madman loose aboard his ship, and that is what he considered The *Valkyrie*: his ship. She was the new flagship of the Luftwaffe's new lighter than air class. He had heard rumors from the men aboard from the famed Condor Squadron that an even larger vessel was being secretly constructed, a true floating airbase that could deliver entire armies to any point on the globe. If the rumors were true, Germany would truly be masters of the skies!

For who would be able to stop the formidable might of the Nazi war machine if they could deliver an entire army anywhere on the globe in two day's time? Not the British, and certainly not their poor upstart cousins the Americans. The Americans were too frightened to even join in the war effort! They made a lot of noise, but even the bloody Brits couldn't talk them into sending men or materials to combat the growing Nazi presence in Europe or their growing conquests.

It would only be a matter of time before Germany ruled the world. And when Germany did, it would be through military might, not through some silly religious hoodoo.

"Wessel," he heard his name spoken in long sibilant snake-like fashion. Hans Wessel turned to see Doctor Ragnarok standing in the doorway of his command room.

"What do you want, Herr Doktor?" Wessel asked sternly, much more sternly than he felt, because the madman before him still frightened him intensely. He had felt the man's power and could sense what sort of Evil he was capable of.

"They are coming, Wessel. Soon they will be within our grasp, and when they are, we will force them to lead us to our prize! They shall lead us to The Emerald of Eternity. Once we have it, no one will stand in our way!" Ragnarok cackled madly, rubbing his gloved hands together.

"How do you know this?" Wessel asked, humoring the mad creature.

"I can feel them, drawing nearer. And He is with them. One I have faced before. This time He shall pay for what He did to me, and He shall pay as no other has by dancing naked in the flames of Hell!" Ragnarok raged.

"Let me know when they are close enough, Herr Doktor, and I will make sure we capture them this time so they will have no choice but to lead us to your precious emerald," Wessel replied with a smile that never touched his eyes.

"Yesssss!" Ragnarok hissed as he moved away from the doorway. Wessel felt a shudder of revulsion pass through him. He almost pitied Ragnarok, who had slid from being a terrifying being to a jabbering madman in just a few hours.

Wessel found himself wondering if the doctor might not just die and save him the trouble of having to kill him once the silly jewel was recovered.

~ ~ ~

Hardluck Hannigan checked the magazine for the MAS 36 Carbine and slapped it into place. He was surprised to find that the good Padre had a couple of the French bolt action rifles at the Mission. They had only been adopted by the French Military the year before, so it was only natural that the Belgians would have them, but for someone as anti-violence as the Padre to have acquired a couple had come as a real shock.

There were a good many layers to the priest's character, Hannigan had discovered, and he was sure he had yet to see them all. He could also sense darkness within the man that few others apparently could see, and it troubled him. McKenzie was a priest, a man of the cloth. Yet there was darkness in his soul that Hannigan found very troubling. Hannigan shook the thought away and went back to examining the rifle.

The MAS 36 carbine fired a 7.5x54mm cartridge and could hold up to 5 rounds in the magazine. It wasn't a Thompson submachine gun by any means, but it had a lot more range to it! He had a feeling that it would come in pretty handy in the area they were heading into.

Hannigan heard the soft scrape of boot leather on gravel behind him and he spun drawing the rifle to his shoulder and flipped off the safety as his finger found the trigger. He found himself looking over the sights at Bridget's suddenly pale face. Hannigan lowered the rifle and blew out a long breath.

"Sneaking up on people isn't a real smart move," Hannigan whispered, his whole body shaking at how close a call it had been.

"I see that, now," Bridget replied, a slight quiver audible in her voice.

"I'm still surprised that your daddy had something like this around. Isn't he afraid it might tempt the natives?" Hannigan asked, abruptly changing the subject. He did not want to think about how close he had come to almost blowing her brains out through the back of her pretty red head.

"I just came to tell you it's time to go. Dad wants you to fly with him; I'll have Gregor and the Italian with me," Bridget spoke quietly. "Besides, if the tribes get restless, we need to be able to defend ourselves as well."

"I guess," was all Hannigan could think to say as Bridget spun on her heel and ran towards the Duck. Hannigan mentally cursed himself as he followed along more slowly. Bridget was already in the Duck and had the engines going by the time he reached the older smaller Great War edition bi-plane. This one just happened to have floats instead of wheels.

"You ready?" McKenzie asked, as taciturn as ever.

"As much as I'll ever be," Hannigan replied. Moments later both planes were climbing up into the blue African sky. Hannigan wondered if the journey would be worth what he had been put through so far.

~ ~ ~

Claude DuChamps climbed out of the airplane and was thankful to be back on the ground once more. Antoine Gerrard and Paul Fontaine followed him from the aircraft. They had come in search of a man, a man worth one hundred thousand dollars American. His name was Mike Hannigan. There had been three other men who had gone looking to collect the price on the American's head, but they had vanished.

Now it was Claude's turn. He would find where the man had gone once he had disembarked from The African Queen. He already had the name of a man to look for, the local center for criminal activity: Francisco Degiorno.

CHAPTER SEVENTEEN

IT DID NOT TAKE LONG for both planes to get into the air. Hannigan was riding with McKenzie this time out and he was troubled by his last encounter with Bridget. Yes he had aimed a weapon at her, but she had snuck up on him, something that by this point, she should know better than to do. However, she might not have realized that she had snuck up on him. There was more than one way to look at it, and Hannigan knew he had to figure out how Bridget had taken it. He shook his head. Women, there wasn't a more complicated species on the planet!

The sun had risen high in the sky and was working its way west. The rush of wind through his hair was much more exhilarating this time since he was actually inside the plane rather than roped to the side of one. On the flight from the boat to the Mission, Bridget had taught him the basics of flying. He had hoped to get time to learn more, but the race for the lost city had taken precedence over a flying lesson.

They were a full day behind the Nazis who by now realized that the map they had was not the original that they had shown Degiorno, but a clever fake that the Italian had managed to slip to them when he had stolen the original. When the Nazis found them, they would not be happy. This was one of the reasons that Hannigan had been so happy to discover the MAS 36 rifles tucked away under lock and key at the Mission. The weapons gave them some range, range that he just didn't have with his beloved Colt. The Colt had been a gift from his father, a weapon his father had carried during the Great War. Back when Wild Bill Hannigan was a member of the famous Fighting Hawks. Hannigan knew he had broken his father's heart when he had run off to see the world. Someday, he knew, he would have to go back and see his father, make amends for leaving the way he had. Hannigan knew that there were probably a lot of things he had to make amends for.

~ ~ ~

Pointe Noire, Congo, Africa

Claude DuChamps looked irritated as he stood at the door of the Broken Tusk. The bar was closed until further notice according to the sign posted on the door. The Frenchman wondered exactly who had closed the bar. Judging from the number of bullet holes in the doors and wall, it had not been a voluntary closing.

DuChamps felt his sense of frustration mounting. According to his contacts in Sicily, this was supposed to be a simple contract. Find one American working for the Italian and kill him. Now both had mysteriously vanished and no one in the port town was talking. Merde!

The situation was intolerable. He had to find out what had happened here the day The African Queen had docked. The big tramp steamer was already gone, but he knew that Mike Hannigan had not been aboard; going after The African Queen would be of no use!

He had sent his two men to search for information about the American, the Broken Tusk and its owner Francisco Degiorno. So far, they had been unable to turn up any information. It was as if Degiorno and Hannigan had both dropped off the face of the earth! Already trouble was brewing in the port town. Degiorno had been a power in the city's underworld; now he was gone and a vacuum was left in his place. Since nature abhors a vacuum, there were any number of candidates struggling to take his place.

~ ~ ~

"There they are!" Ragnarok pointed suddenly towards two small black specks that had appeared in the sky over the verdant green foliage of the jungle. They were barely even visible to the naked eye.

"How can you be sure?" Hans Wessel asked cautiously.

"I can feel Him!" Ragnarok hissed, his voice sounding even more reptilian than before.

"Feel who?" Wessel's curiosity getting the better of him.

"Him! The one who did this to me, who trapped me in this pathetic shell! Revenge is coming soon, " Ragnarok croaked.

"This person is also after The Emerald of Eternity?" Wessel asked softly, still trying to elicit information.

"Yes you fool! Haven't you been listening? I said He was coming! Pay attention!" Ragnarok admonished.

Hans Wessel sat back wondering exactly who the mysterious He was. The man obviously had Ragnarok rattled, and rattled deeply.

~ ~ ~

Niles McKenzie felt a chill race down his spine as the biplane sped over the emerald expanse of the jungle. He closed his eyes and reached out, trying to pinpoint what had caused the chill. He sensed a presence, somewhat familiar yet darkly evil. He had faced it before, he knew it. Then it came to him in a flash. Doctor Ragnarok! The last time he had faced him was aboard a ship full of hostages near the end of the Great War.

McKenzie had thought that the evil wizard had died when he had plunged off the rail of the ship, engulfed in the blue fire of magic. His heart skipped a beat as he realized that he had been so wrong. Fear clutched as his gut as he realized that not only would he be facing the wrath of Prester John, but of the evil Doctor Ragnarok as well.

McKenzie shook his head, knowing that what lay ahead of him would be perhaps the most dangerous battle he would ever face. Just then bullets shredded through the wings of the biplane!

~ ~ ~

Hardluck Hannigan flinched as he saw the fabric along the left wing of the bi-plane explode into wood and cloth particles. Hannigan jerked his head around to look over his shoulder. Two Messerschmitt fighter planes were diving on them from above, guns blazing. Instinctively his hand went for the Colt on his waist, then he realized that the small bi-plane had a machine gun. Hannigan grabbed the grips on the gun and aimed at the attacking fighters, his finger tightening on the twin triggers.

The machine gun roared and bucked in his fists as tracers blazed back towards the German fighter planes. Flame erupted from the engine compartment of the nearer fighter and the plane veered off, trailing smoke. Hannigan started humming to himself as he tracked the remaining fighter against the broad expanse of blue sky. It took him a moment to realize he was humming Glenn Miller's Pennsylvania 6-5000 as he tracked the German fighter across the sky.

The second ship went into a roll, trying to avoid the stream of tracers but with no real success. Flames exploded from the wings and the German ship roared down in a smoke trailed arc to the jungle below. Flame and debris erupted in a small black mushroom cloud climbing from the vast expanse of green.

Hannigan looked back and saw Bridget pulling slightly ahead of them as a long silvery cigar shape descended from the wispy white clouds above. Hannigan recognized it immediately as the large silver zeppelin that he had spotted the night that The African Queen had arrived in Africa.

The Nazis had found them! Suddenly more fighters emerged from the rear of the zeppelin. "How?" Hannigan growled as he swung the guns around, firing them out at the approaching fighters. Two more started trailing smoke and went crashing into the jungle below. The same jungle, Hannigan noted that was rushing up to greet them. "Padre, what the heck are you thinking?" Hannigan yelled, his stomach suddenly flipping over.

"Evasive action!" McKenzie's voice drifted back to him over the screaming of the engine. Seemingly at the last possible instant, McKenzie pulled out of the dive and Hannigan could see leaves and branches flying into the air as they were broken off by the bi-plane's undercarriage.

"Holy Cow!" Hannigan exclaimed as one of the attacking planes that had been on their tail hit the trees and exploded in a ball of flames. He drew his beloved .45 and aimed it at one of the approaching Messerschmitt fighters. Thumbing off the safety he lined up the sights and pulled the trigger. He saw the cockpit glass spider-web and the pilot jerk backwards. The nose of the plane lifted and the plane piloted by a dead man plowed into the underbelly of another fighter that was using its machineguns to chew up the bi-plane's wings. The shockwave from the explosion proved too much, however, and it slammed the undercarriage of the bi-plane down into the verdant expanse of trees. The ship lurched hard and something slammed into Mike Hannigan's head, sending him dropping into a deep dark pit.

~ ~ ~

Bridget felt her heart lurch into her throat as she saw the other bi-plane go down into the jungle. The only saving grace was that she saw no flames, so the bi-plane had not exploded. That meant that there was still a chance that her adopted father and Hardluck Hannigan had survived! The survival of the Duck was a wholly different matter. Two of the fighters sent tracers across her path and Bridget began searching for someplace to set the Duck down. She didn't want bullet holes in her precious plane. The Duck was almost a physical extension of her body. The plane responded to her lightest touch and in seconds she was setting the floatplane down on a tributary of the Congo. The huge silver zeppelin dropped down to hover above the Duck. Lines dropped from the gondola and men began rappelling to the ground. They were all heavily armed.

"We may be in trouble," Bridget told her passengers.

"You think?" Gregor Shotsky asked innocently as he climbed out of the plane. Francisco Degiorno had to be bodily removed and he dropped to his knees in pure fear as a man in a silver-colored metal mask approached them.

"You!" the man in the metal mask hissed as he saw Degiorno. The Italian curled into a ball, the scent of his fear heavy in the air. "Where is the real map?" the man demanded.

"Locked in my safe," Degiorno replied.

"You will lead us to the emerald or I will make sure you suffer more than if you were on the lowest level of hell," the man in the metal mask said.

"I believe you," the Italian gasped, his fear so strong it could almost be tasted in the air.

"You really are a poor excuse for a man," Bridget told the Italian.

Degiorno gave her a highly insulting Italian gesture. Bridget laughed despite the situation. Deep inside, she was holding onto the hope that both Hannigan and her adoptive father had survived the crash.

~ ~ ~

Mike Hannigan opened his eyes. Somehow the plane had lodged itself in the upper branches of a large tree. McKenzie was still slumped over the controls of the plane in the forward compartment. Hannigan found his beloved .45 on the floorboards. He buttoned out the partially spent magazine and slammed a full one into place. He would take the time to reload the partially spent magazine.

Several minutes later, Hannigan dragged Niles McKenzie from the cockpit of the bi-plane. The branches were thick so he was easily able to maneuver the unconscious priest out of the plane and close to the bole of the tree. Father McKenzie was his only real lead to reach the kingdom of the Priest King Prester John. He had to make sure McKenzie could get him there!

CHAPTER EIGHTEEN

GREGOR SHOTSKY LIFTED HIS HEAD, sweat streaming down his face, eyes slit to the point that they were barely open. Pain exploded from nearly every part of his body, an after effect of the interrogation he had suffered at the hands of the fiend who called himself Doctor Ragnarok. The name was a term he was familiar with; it translated into another word in English: Armageddon. The end of all life on Earth. Shotsky had no doubt that Ragnarok would bring that about if he got his hands on the Emerald of Eternity.

Shotsky held onto the hope that Mike 'Hardluck' Hannigan would reach them in time, before the creature working for the Nazis got his hands on the stone. Every inch of his body ached and he had listened as Francisco Degiorno had suffered the tortures of the damned during his interrogation. The Italian lay against the wall, his eyes blank, drool running from the corners of his mouth. Whatever mind Degiorno had possessed before the interrogation, Shotsky was willing to bet it had been totally shattered by the techniques used by Ragnarok.

His main concern for the moment was how Bridget was faring in Ragnarok's hands. Hannigan was in love with Bridget. If anything bad happened to her, he knew he would not be able to control his young American friend, nor would he be able to control the priest that had adopted Bridget as a child of his own. Together, Shotsky had a pretty good impression that they would be unstoppable, especially if Bridget were in danger. He hoped that Ragnarok would recognize that fact as well and take it easy on her. A scream ripped the air from the compartment where Ragnarok was interrogating Bridget. The Russian tore at his bonds, struggling to free himself, but to no avail. A long silence descended, and Gregor Shotsky feared the worst.

~ ~ ~

Bridget Ellen O'Malley struggled against the ropes that bound her hands behind her back. She had to find a way to escape. Their captors had separated her from the others. Her stomach churned with fear at the thought of what could be done to her. Then the door to the room she was in opened and a man with a metal mask walked in. She looked up as he took the mask off and couldn't help herself. The sight of his horribly scarred face made her let loose with a horrified scream.

"Yesssss, child, scream to your heart's content. Let the others hear you, let them imagine you in intense pain, tortured beyond belief," Ragnarok cackled insanely.

"Who are you?" Bridget whispered, her voice almost catching in her throat.

"My name, child, is Doctor Ragnarok. I'm an old acquaintance of Niles McKenzie. You are familiar with him I believe?"

"He's my adoptive father," Bridget replied before she could stop herself. Despite of, or maybe because of, his hideous appearance, she felt compelled to answer him truthfully.

"Your father. How interesting," Ragnarok gloated, rubbing his gloved hands together.

"What do you want with him?" Bridget demanded, some of her fear fading, being replaced with anger and wanting to protect her adopted father.

"What do I want? Niles McKenzie was the one who did this to me! Him and that thrice damned Dane Hawkins!" Ragnarok roared. "Perhaps I should do some work on that pretty face of yours and see how Daddy Dearest likes it!" Ragnarok said, starting towards her.

Bridget screamed again, this time the terror in her voice unmistakable.

~ ~ ~

Hardluck Hannigan looked up, his blue eyes frosting up to a polar glare as he heard the distant scream of terror. He was carrying Niles McKenzie across his shoulders as he made his way through the jungle via the large interlocking tree branches. He recognized the voice and the scream. It was Bridget. She was in terrible danger!

Steeling his resolve, he knew he had to put McKenzie in a safe place. He tied the priest to the bole of a tree and started to climb. Several moments later he could look through the foliage and see the huge silver zeppelin. It appeared to be less than a mile away. Hannigan was torn. He didn't want to leave McKenzie, yet he had to do something to rescue Bridget from the Nazis. Hannigan worked his way back down the tree to where McKenzie was roped in place. The priest was showing signs of regaining consciousness at last. Hannigan knelt beside him.

"McKenzie, wake up!" his said, slapping the man's face lightly. McKenzie's eyes fluttered open.

"What happened?" McKenzie asked weakly, shaking his head.

"Bad landing," Hannigan replied with a grin.

"Why am I tied up, Hannigan?" McKenzie asked softly.

"To keep you from falling outta this tree for one thing," Hannigan replied, drawing a knife he had picked up at the Mission and cutting through the knots he had tied earlier. A moment later the priest was free.

"Bridget and the others?" McKenzie asked, becoming more alert with each passing moment.

"The Nazis have them. The zeppelin is about a mile ahead of us as the crow flies. Got any ideas on how we can free them?" Hannigan asked.

"Maybe. How did we get this far from the crash?" McKenzie asked.

"I carried you on my back as I ran along the tree branches. You're awake now so I'm not doing that anymore. You're heavier than you look, Padre," Hannigan said.

"On a positive note, we're just outside the domain of Prester John. I hope we can free the others before we have to face him and his army. I don't want to have to battle the Nazis and him at the same time," McKenzie said. His face was even paler than usual, Hannigan noted.

"You sure you're up to this, Padre?" Hannigan asked. He had no desire to nursemaid the priest if it meant he might not be able to rescue Bridget.

"It's for Bridget, I have no choice but to be up for it," McKenzie replied.

"Then we had better get moving," Hannigan said. Turning, he started along the branch. He heard McKenzie hesitate, then take a deep breath and let it out. A moment later he could feel the priest starting to race along behind him.

Running through the trees, leaping from branch to branch over dizzying heights, Hannigan forced himself to focus on getting to Bridget. If he thought about what he was doing, he would end up missing his target and breaking his neck falling to the jungle floor. So instead, he focused on the girl he loved, the girl who was in deadly danger from the Nazis.

When he had first arrived in Africa, Hannigan hadn't been sure what direction his life was about to take. Since meeting Bridget, he had found a focus. He knew what he wanted to do. He would help fight for those who were oppressed, fight on the side of the underdogs in the third world countries. Slavery abounded in Africa thanks to colonizers like the Belgium people; they maimed and brutalized the natives, forcing them to work on the rubber plantations. Some of the more war-like tribes still resisted, but they were the exception, not the rule. In Africa, home of the Negro race, the natives were still treated as second-class citizens. It was something that Hannigan found appalling on a very personal level. All men had the right to live free with a measure of dignity. Mike "Hardluck" Hannigan took a moment then to vocalize his future. "A soldier of fortune," he whispered as he ran.

It sounded almost silly when he verbalized it, yet he knew it was the correct choice. Suddenly, he could see daylight ahead of him through a clearing in the trees, and ropes dangling from above. They had reached the zeppelin. Hannigan slid to a halt near the end of the branch he had been running on. He glanced behind him at McKenzie.

"We're here," Hannigan whispered. The priest nodded, his shirt soaked from exertion, his pallor worse.

"How do we get to them?" McKenzie asked. He was breathing even more heavily than Hannigan, practically wheezing with the effort it was taking to regain his breath.

"We don't, not right away. We watch, we learn, and then we plan and execute it," Hannigan replied. McKenzie nodded in agreement. Hannigan was actually surprised that the Padre wasn't insisting on taking the lead on rescuing Bridget. She was, after all, his daughter and he was the one with all the experience according to the folk at the Mission.

The Priest was making a habit of surprising him, and Hannigan wasn't sure that he liked it. He didn't trust anyone so full of surprises. They might surprise you at the wrong time in the wrong way, which could prove deadly.

~ ~ ~

Gregor Shotsky looked up as Bridget O'Malley staggered back into the room, tripping and falling onto the floor of the cabin. "Bridget! Are you okay?" Gregor asked urgently.

"Yes, God he was horrible looking!" she gasped, pushing herself up and brushing the hair from her face.

"He?" Gregor asked. He had almost managed to free his hands. The Nazis had missed a small folding knife he had tucked under his belt and he had gotten it out and managed to open the blade, using it to saw through the rough hemp ropes.

"That horrible man! He called himself Doctor Ragnarok! He claims to know my father, and that Dad is responsible for his horrible burns. He seems to be their leader," Bridget replied.

"Ragnarok? I've heard stories about him. He was some sort of bigwig during the Great War. Ragnarok was finally taken down by the Fighting Hawks. Wait a minute! Bridget, are you telling me that the Padre is that Niles McKenzie? The one that fought alongside Captain Dane Hawkins?"

"He was with Captain Hawkins, Devil Dog and the rest. But from what he says, he was the Chaplin for the unit," Bridget replied, surprise written across her expression.

"Chaplin? Niles McKenzie was much more than that, Bridget. He was a spiritual advisor sure, but also an expert on the Occult. He was one of the core members of the Fighting Hawks! Which means he probably did all Ragnarok said and more. We heard of the Hawks even in Russia. They were great men, fearless and capable, who fought like demons and gave no quarter. They lost a lot of men, but they always emerged victorious," Gregor replied as the last rope snapped across the cutting edge of the knife's blade.

"I know Dad was in the war, Gregor, but are you sure about all of this?" Bridget asked, her voice still carrying signs of doubt. Shotsky tossed the ropes that had bound his hands away and started sawing at the ones around his ankles.

"I am very sure, Bridget. But I know one other thing that even Michael doesn't know. His father knew your father! They were both a part of the Flying Hawks. Look closely at the .45 that Hannigan carries. The slide has an inscription engraved into it. 'To Wild Bill Hannigan for special services, Dane Hawkins.' I have read the inscription, Bridget. You all were linked years before either of you was born," Shotsky told her.

"That's impossible, Gregor. You're making it sound as if all that has happened was predestined," Bridget told him, climbing to her feet.

"Can you honestly say it was not?" Gregor asked her as the last strand of rope parted. He kicked off the ropes and sprang to his feet. The knife went back into hiding. There was always a chance that he might need it again. They heard footsteps outside the door. Shotsky flattened himself against the bulkhead next to the hatch. It swung open and one of the khaki-clad Nazis entered the room, an MP-36 submachine gun slung from his shoulder. Bridget waved him on in and Shotsky slammed both fists into the back of the man's head dropping him like a pole axed steer.

The Nazi crumpled to the deck but Shotsky was there, catching him and easing him down so he didn't make any noise. Bridget moved forward quickly, taking the soldier's Lugar P-08 9mm pistol and the spare magazines from his belt. She worked the safety on the pistol after making sure it had a round chambered and stuffed it into her waistband. The spare magazines went into her trouser pockets. Shotsky availed himself of the sub gun and the extra magazines for it. Now at least they had a fighting chance.

Gregor had no idea how they were going to get off the zeppelin, but he knew they would go down fighting at least! He looked at Bridget. "Got any ideas how we might get off of this thing?" She looked back at him for a moment and then nodded.

"Maybe," she replied then she eased open the door. The corridor was empty. "We might have a chance if we can reach the cargo hold," she whispered.

"Exactly where might that be?" Gregor snorted, unconvinced.

"Just down this corridor if I remember the article I read about these lighter than air craft," Bridget replied winking at him.

"Article?" Shotsky asked, puzzled.

"Yeah, aircraft are one thing I keep up on. I get all the latest aviation magazines and journals at the Mission. Got to keep up with what's going on in the world," Bridget whispered mischievously.

"You mean you read about this zeppelin in some magazine article? One of the Nazi's best kept secrets?" Gregor asked, amazed as they reached the hatch and Bridget threw it open.

"You would be surprised at the information available in the latest scientific journals devoted to the subject," Bridget replied, stepping into the hold. Her eyes swept the room, searching for something specific.

"Amazing," Shotsky replied, shaking his head. Just then their luck ran out and a loud voice shouted at them from the other end of the corridor.

"HALT!" shouted the voice.

"Hannigan's luck is sure rubbing off!" Gregor growled spinning as he tensioned the sub gun against the sling, his fingers flipping off the safety and squeezing the trigger in one quick motion. The MP-36 in his fists roared a stuttered burst as he worked the trigger, going for three and four shot semi-auto bursts. He knew he only had a finite amount of ammunition and he planned on conserving it as long as he could. The man at the end of the corridor went down in a bloody heap but now everyone aboard would know that they were free.

"Here we go!" Bridget called, shoving open a panel to reveal the outside.

"Okay, you found a hatch. We're still a hundred yards or better off the ground," Gregor growled, firing at two more of the Nazis that had entered the corridor. So far they were withholding from firing back, but he was pretty sure that wasn't going to last.

"That's what this is for," Bridget replied kicking a huge coil of rope out the hatch and watching as it uncoiled while falling towards the ground.

"You are insane!" Gregor snapped, firing the MP-36 again.

"Got a better idea?" Bridget asked. She had found a blanket and wrapped it around her hands. She flashed him a smile then disappeared out the hatch, sliding down the rope towards the jungle below.

"God save me from crazy people!" Gregor growled as he quickly wrapped several layers of cloth around his own hands and swung out the hatch, catching the rope and letting gravity do its thing.

CHAPTER NINETEEN

MIKE HANNIGAN LOOKED ON in shock as Bridget and Gregor dived out of the bottom of the gondola below the zeppelin. "Okay, change of plans!" he snapped as he ran out into the clearing. Bridget and Gregor were sliding down ropes and he could see smoke streaming out around their hands. He hoped they were protected or their skin would be filleted through by the ropes from the friction.

Hannigan leveled the MAS 36 he had brought from the wreckage of the plane and fired at the zeppelin, at the men hanging out the hatch firing at Bridget and Gregor. He was rewarded by a body tumbling out the hatch and plummeting towards the ground, quickly passing the pair since it was free falling. The dead Nazi splashed into the earth with a wet thud.

Bridget dropped to the ground and rolled away from the bottom of the rope. Gregor hit seconds behind her. "Run for the trees!" Hannigan screamed at them both. They scrambled across the ground, heading for the undergrowth. Hannigan fired a few more rounds and ran after them, McKenzie trailing along behind him.

"Good work, you two," Hannigan told them.

"Thanks, Hardluck," Bridget grinned.

"Your Hardluck seems to be rubbing off, Michael," Shotsky told him as they gained the cover of the trees.

"It happens, pal," Hannigan grinned.

"So it does. Michael, your father was a companion of Niles McKenzie and Captain Hawkins. Were you aware of this?" Gregor asked as they moved deeper into the jungle.

"I knew he knew Hawkins," Hannigan replied grimly.

"McKenzie was one of Hawkins' most trusted companions during the Great War," Gregor explained.

"Interesting," Hannigan replied. He didn't really like talking about his father. As much as he loved and respected him, Wild Bill Hannigan had thought he should remain in Greensboro, Indiana, a small town farm boy. Hannigan had known that remaining in Indiana had not been his destiny, however.

"You're Wild Bill's boy?" McKenzie asked suddenly from behind them.

"Eavesdropping, Padre?" Hannigan asked, raising an eyebrow.

"Not at all," McKenzie replied.

~ ~ ~

"What is happening?" Wessel demanded, running down the corridor to the cargo bay.

"The prisoners are escaping!" one of his men shouted back.

"Stop them!" Wessel ordered.

"We've lost two men already, and the prisoners have already made it into the jungle," one of his men replied.

"Go after them! Now! All available personnel after the prisoners," Wessel commanded.

"I will lead them," hissed a voice from behind him. Wessel spun around only to find Ragnarok filling the doorway. No longer was he bent and pitiful. Ragnarok was once more standing tall and brimming with strength. Wessel was puzzled. What could have brought about such a change so quickly?

"Never underestimate my power, Captain. We are close to the Emerald of Eternity. Our goals are almost achieved. The only man who might possibly stop me is now ahead of us. Lower this ship so we can catch them. The airship is no longer of any use," Ragnarok announced firmly.

"As you wish, Herr Doktor," Wessel replied, maintaining his stance. He brushed past the ancient wizard

144

and headed for the control center. Wessel was aware of Ragnarok's laughter following him.

~ ~ ~

"How far to this lost city, Padre?" Hannigan asked coldly. He was angry at McKenzie, but he wasn't about to let the man know how angry he was. Not with the Nazis on their tail. Hannigan still didn't trust McKenzie not to betray them all at some point.

"Not far. In fact, we already have an escort," McKenzie said quietly.

"What?" Hannigan asked, surprised by the comment. Suddenly men in ancient armor were stepping out of the underbrush. Hannigan counted at least twenty. He and Gregor might be able to take out several of them, but not before they finally fell under the blades of the swords and spears that the men carried.

"Part of the army of Prester John," McKenzie replied. One of the men picked that moment to step forward and bark a command at them in a language that Hannigan couldn't understand. McKenzie rattled off some sort of reply, gesturing behind them.

"It's ancient Latin, Hannigan," Bridget explained, looking a little awestruck.

"Can you understand what they are saying?" Hannigan whispered.

"Yes. Dad is telling them about the Nazis and that Horrible Doctor Ragnarok," Bridget whispered. Suddenly the man McKenzie was speaking with straightened. He motioned for them all to follow him as he began to trot off down a well-worn jungle path. "He told them Ragnarok is after the gemstone," Bridget said grimly.

"What did he tell them about us?" Hannigan asked, falling into a trot.

"Not much," Bridget replied, trotting beside him.
"Specifics, Bridget," Hannigan demanded, noting her sudden evasiveness.

"He told them that you and Gregor are also after the stone, and that he and I have come to help protect it," Bridget almost choked on the words.

"I knew he wasn't playing it straight," Hannigan growled, his face darkening.

"Mike, what are you going to do?" Bridget asked, worry tingeing her words.

"You'll know when the time comes," Hannigan replied.

"Hannigan," Bridget began, but Hannigan was pulling ahead of her. She found herself wondering if she had not just lost him because of her father.

~ ~ ~

Stepping onto the jungle floor, Ragnarok could feel the power of the Emerald of Eternity pulsing through the very earth itself. The closer he came to it, the more strength he drew from the gemstone. His power was growing as he drew nearer. Niles McKenzie was not far ahead of his group. When he caught up to McKenzie, he would have his revenge!"

~ ~ ~

Hans Wessel watched as Ragnarok disappeared into the jungle with two full squads of his men. The wizard thought that the *Valkyrie* was out of the action. He was about to find out how wrong he was. Wessel turned to his second in command, Heinrich Dieter. "Send out Alpha Squad. Acquire the emerald and kill Ragnarok. Call us when you have the stone and we will drop in and pull you out," Wessel commanded.

"It shall be done," Dieter snapped off a salute and spun on his heel, hurrying off to do his captain's biding. Wessel watched him go, then turned and headed for the radio room. He had to make contact with the Kondor Legion and update them on his mission.

~ ~ ~

"McKenzie sold us out," Hannigan whispered to Gregor Shotsky as he jogged along next to him.

"How?" Shotsky asked, trying to save his breath for running. He had spent a long time aboard ship and all the sudden exercise was catching up with him.

"Bridget was able to translate what McKenzie told that guy. He told them that we were after the stone as well as the Nazis and that he was here to protect it," Hannigan explained.

"I'll be ready then, Hardluck. Even now, your luck shapes you," Gregor said, managing a grin despite the situation.

"That's the way it goes. Just be ready when the opportunity arises," Hannigan said, slowly dropping back from Shotsky.

Several minutes later they entered a larger path, this one paved with cut stones. Shortly after, they emerged into a clearing and what they saw took their breath away.

~ ~ ~

He had visitors. The first in several years. He had felt their approach from the moment they had entered his domain. One of them he recognized immediately. The Emissary from Rome, and three others. Another group followed behind them. He stretched out his senses, searching for information. Lost souls, the last group, and one being of pure Evil. He ran his fingers through his silver hair and walked across the room.

It had been nearly a millennium since he had first come to the Dark Continent and established his kingdom, following the precepts and teachings of the one called Jesus of Nazareth, the Christ. It was the Christ who had told him where to find the stone, the emerald that had allowed his kingdom to prosper and grow. It had allowed him to fulfill his vision and establish a Christian Kingdom among the unbelievers.

His men had stood against all who had tried to invade his kingdom. They stood strong against the assassins sent by those in Rome who feared him and the power he possessed. They feared the time when he would march out of the jungle to do battle with the false prophet, the son of the Deceiver.

He realized that the Emissary had led the soulless one to him. The demonic entity that craved the fabled stone. He could read through the shallow desire of the Emissary's heart as easy as any other mans. The Emissary hoped that he and the Soulless one would battle to the death and that the Emissary would be able to take the Emerald of Eternity back to the pretenders in Rome.

Prester John lifted his crown from the table and placed it on his head. It was time to meet his guests. Both groups. Smiling to himself, Prester John left his personal quarters and walked to the throne room.

~ ~ ~

Heinrich Dieter and his men moved through the jungle like ghosts. They had trained in this sort of environment before, trained to be able to move unseen by any watchers, to surround, infiltrate and destroy anyone who opposed them. He was sure Ragnarok was unaware that they followed. The madman was too focused on the emerald and the person he called McKenzie to worry that Wessel might be acting against him. They had seen signs of native watchers, but had slipped past them unnoticed as well. Soon they would reach the fabled lost city and then it would be time to kill Ragnarok and recover the gemstone.

~ ~ ~

Hannigan was impressed by the opulence of the throne room. The city itself had been a marvel to behold, carved

148

from living stone; there was not a single seam between the rocks that formed walls and doorways. In fact the walls appeared to be some sort of quartz, almost pink in nature but the color fluctuated with the light. High windows allowed plenty of sunlight to penetrate the interior, and Hannigan spotted more than one mirror reflecting light to other parts, lighting the interior as brightly as the day outside.

The escort had moved in tighter around them, and he noted the positions of the guards that were closest to him and how they were armed. They were, he deduced, about to meet the famous (or infamous, depending on your point of view) Prester John. The one thing working for Hannigan was the fact that McKenzie feared Prester John, and he had seen little else that the turncoat priest did fear.

The group was herded in front of a raised dais with a marble throne sitting atop it. A curtain behind the throne parted and a most amazing looking man stepped out from behind it. He stood well over six feet tall, his hair almost silver in color, contrasting greatly with his dark bronze colored skin and strong muscled body. Bright blue eyes carried an aura of vitality despite the impressing of great age that hovered over the man. The head of the escort stepped forward and barked out a few words of the language that Bridget had identified as ancient Latin. The new arrival listened intently and nodded. It was then that Hannigan noted the gemstone hanging around the man's neck. It was a beautifully carved emerald square that flashed with an inner light. It could only be the prize they were trying to keep from the Nazis. The fabled Emerald of Eternity!

"Greetings, welcome to my home," the man announced in perfect modern day English. It caught Hannigan by surprise.

"Greetings, Prester John," Niles McKenzie said, taking a step forward.

"Emissary, it has been awhile since you last journeyed to my kingdom. What brings you here?" Prester John asked his eyes burrowing into McKenzie. Hannigan half-smiled as the priest flinched under that direct gaze.

"There are evil men coming who wish to steal your greatest treasure," McKenzie announced.

"Evil is always drawn to power, Emissary," Prester John replied, his voice low and melodic.

"And the Emissary is just as bad as the others that are coming," Mike Hannigan interjected, stepping forward.

"Who are you?" Prester John asked.

"The name is Hannigan. I'm a guy who is here to stop the bad guys from getting their hands on the stone around your neck, even if it means stealing it. It's of no value to me, but both the Catholic Church and the Nazis want the stone for its power. My only goal is to deny that to them, sir. Look into my heart, my soul, and see if I am not telling you the truth," Hannigan said boldly.

"Now see here, Hannigan," McKenzie started. Prester John cut him off.

"Silence, Emissary! I shall do as he asks. If he speaks the truth, he has nothing to fear. If he lies, or there is any deceit in what he says, he will burn in the flames of hellfire," The Priest-king said. "Come forward, Hannigan."

Mike Hannigan stepped forward, closer to the man called Prester John. The Priest King reached out and touched his forehead. Hannigan felt a strange warmth wash over him, a sense of peace and well-being filled him. Hannigan felt the hand of Prester John move to his chest for a brief moment. Then the touch was gone and the warm feeling faded. Hannigan took a deep breath and let it out slowly, then opened his eyes.

"You spoke the truth, Michael Hannigan. Named after the Archangel, you are. And so shall you be. You, Emissary, however spoke only in half-truths and lies. You must suffer for your sins!" Prester John said, turning his attention to McKenzie.

Suddenly gunfire erupted and the escorts started to fall.

Mike Hannigan dived to the ground, slamming his shoulder into Bridget to knock her out of the line of fire as well.

CHAPTER TWENTY

HANNIGAN GRABBED BRIDGET and rolled with her behind the edge of the dais. He peered over the edge. Prester John stood unharmed and totally relaxed as the Nazi invaders stormed into the room. Ragnarok walked in behind them, strong and powerful.

"I am here for The Emerald of Eternity!" Ragnarok announced as he stepped up to face Prester John.

"I know you, Creature of the Void," Prester John replied calmly. The air seemed to almost thicken around the two beings. Hannigan shook his head. Beings fit more than men, because he was quite sure neither of them was truly human, not anymore.

"How do you know me, human scum?" Ragnarok sounded surprised.

"I have seen the faces of every demon spawned in Hell. I have sent many of your kind back to your dark master," Prester John replied.

"You will send me nowhere, human scum. But I will have the Emerald of Eternity!" Ragnarok said.

"Oh really?" Prester John asked, sounding more than slightly amused.

"I got a feeling this is about to get really ugly," Hannigan said, his tone hushed.

"I've got to get to Dad," Bridget said, pushing to her hands and knees.

"Bridget, out there is the last place you need to go," Hannigan said, his hand on her shoulder. Bridget threw his hand off.

"I have to save Dad," Bridget said, her voice suddenly cold. She crawled off towards where Niles McKenzie had fallen

"That girl is too damned headstrong for her own good," Hannigan muttered to himself.

Blue energy was crackling around the form of Doctor Ragnarok. A green glow surrounded Prester John. "This can't be good," Gregor Shotsky said from his side. Hannigan hadn't even noticed his old friend reaching his side.

"I agree, old friend," Hannigan said. "What do we do now?"

"Find a way out of here," Shotsky suggested.

"No can do, pal, at least I can't. I have to find a way to keep that weirdo in the metal mask from getting that gemstone," Hannigan replied. Energy beams were crackling between Prester John and Ragnarok. While they appeared evenly matched, Hannigan wasn't so sure that was true. Ragnarok seemed to be absorbing more energy than he was putting out, yet Prester John appeared to be weakening.

"How can we help him?" Shotsky asked with a sigh.

"We've gotta find a way to disrupt whatever Ragnarok's doing," Hannigan said, his eyes searching the room.

"How do you propose we do that?" Shotsky asked.

"Those things you made at the Mission, where are they?" Hannigan asked, the germ of an idea forming.

"Yes, here," Shotsky handed him one.
"Give me the rundown on how to work it again," Hannigan said, not taking his eyes off the two combatants. "Fast!"

The energy crackling out from Ragnarok was now a dark blue, almost black as it lashed at the fading green glow surrounding Prester John. The Priest-king was fading fast. They had to help him or all would be lost!

"Twist the end loose, then hit that small button just below the threads," Shotsky explained. Hannigan's hands were already in motion, twisting the top of the club-like device loose. He pointed it at Ragnarok and hit the button. There was a loud twang as a strongly coiled spring released and the top half of the club shot forward like a rocket. The metal club hit the energy field surrounding Ragnarok, then struck his helmet. White light exploded from the ancient wizard, lashing out like lightning throughout the room. Stones exploded from the wall, crashing down around them all.

Bright green light flared up after the white light had dimmed. Green fire exploded around Ragnarok, burning him. The metal of his mask smoked as he screamed within it, and then began to turn red and melt. Mike Hannigan watched as Bridget and McKenzie scrambled out towards the front entrance that they had entered by. He looked at Gregor Shotsky. "The curtain behind the throne. It's our only hope!" he shouted. Together they ran through the entrance. The whole building was shaking, chunks of stone were tumbling from both walls and ceiling

Running down the corridor, they searched frantically for an exit. Gregor spotted the opening first and dragged him towards it. Both men dived out into the open as a loud rumble sounded from behind them and the lost city began to collapse with a thunderous roar. A thick cloud of dust rose up into the air.

"Your luck, Michael, it holds true to form," Gregor chuckled as he rolled to a sitting position. Hannigan looked over his shoulder.

"Everybody's a critic," Hannigan growled.

"Yes well at least we are alive," Gregor said.

"That should count for something," Hannigan agreed.

"Halt! Put your hands behind your heads!" ordered a voice with a thick German accent.

"Aw crap!" Hannigan said.

"Hardluck or no luck," Shotsky sighed.

~ ~ ~

Bridget looked up as the dust cloud rose into the air. 'Hannigan," she gasped. She started towards the rubble but Niles McKenzie grabbed her shoulder, drawing her back.

"He's gone, Bridget," McKenzie said. She felt tears coursing down her cheeks, cutting tracks through the dust

"He can't be gone, Dad, I love him," Bridget sobbed. She felt his arms tighten around her.

"I'm sorry Bridget," Niles McKenzie said, and for her sake, he truly meant it. Neither of them noticed the silver zeppelin pass overhead. Bridget stayed in her father's embrace for a long time. Finally he let her go and together they started back to where she had landed the Duck.

~ ~ ~

Hans Wessel looked at the two prisoners that his men had recovered. From what they had told him, the Emerald of Eternity had been lost when the lost city had collapsed, taking Ragnarok with it. Ragnarok was no loss, but the emerald was. No matter, at least he had the two prisoners to deliver to the Kondor Legion.

To be continued in *The Sky Masters*.

ABOUT THE AUTHOR

Bill Craig is the best-selling author of more than 60 novels spread across the genres from mystery to pulp to science fiction to westerns. Bill is best known for his *Marlow Key West* mysteries and his *Mitch Cooper* mysteries. Bill often likes to say that it only took him 34 years to become an overnight success. And when introducing himself he adds that he kills people for a living, much like the fictional Rick Castle on television

ABSOLUTELY AMA⚡ING eBOOKS

AbsolutelyAmazingEbooks.com
or AA-eBooks.com